Contents

Threads gathered up

A sequel to "Virgie's Inheritance"

Mrs. Georgie Sheldon

Alpha Editions

This edition published in 2023

ISBN : 9789357944892

Design and Setting By
Alpha Editions
www.alphaedis.com
Email - info@alphaedis.com

CHAPTER I.
AN UNEXPECTED VISITOR.

Three years passed, and nothing occurred to disturb the even tenor of Virgie's life.

She had worked diligently during this time, gaining fresh laurels with every season. She had removed from the retired lodgings which she had taken at first upon coming to San Francisco, into a better locality, where she had a handsome suite of rooms in a well-known apartment-house.

These were bright and pleasant, tastefully furnished also, and Virgie thoroughly enjoyed the pretty home which she had won by the labor of her own hands.

When she had made the change she gave the contents of her other home to Chi Lu, who had married a thrifty woman of his own country, and together they were carrying on quite a flourishing laundry business, while, in place of the faithful Chinese, Virgie had taken a bright and capable Swedish woman.

One evening, after a dreary, rainy day, the bell under the name of "Alexander," in the house of which we have been speaking, was pulled by a vigorous hand.

Virgie was in her chamber, putting her little girl to bed—a service which she enjoyed, for the child always expected a merry frolic and then some "pretty story before the dustman came."

She heard the bell, and soon after voices in the pretty parlor leading from her chamber, and she wondered who could have chosen such a stormy night to call up her, for she seldom had visitors, even in pleasant weather.

Presently Mina, the Swede, came to her, and said that a gentleman was waiting to see her.

"Who is he? Did he give no name?" Virgie questioned, surprised.

"No, madam. I asked him, and he said there was no need to take his name, for you would know him when you saw him."

Virgie's heart beat more quickly at this, and a feeling of dread took possession of her.

Mr. Knight came to see her occasionally, and one or two of his clerks had been there a few times on business, but Mina knew them, so she was sure it was none of these, but someone who must have known her in the past.

She finished the story she was telling little Virgie, made some trifling changes in her toilet, and then went into the parlor.

A gentleman was seated by the table, with his back toward her, and though he had on a heavy overcoat, and his form was considerably bowed, and his hair very gray, there was something familiar about him that sent a sudden shock through Virgie's frame.

As she went forward to greet him he suddenly arose and turned toward her, bending a pair of piercing black eyes searchingly upon her face.

Virgie stopped short as she met that glance, all the color leaving her face, while a startled cry escaped her lips.

The man flushed, and his eyes sank guiltily before hers as he said, in a low tone:

"You know me, then, Virgie?"

"Uncle Mark!" she gasped, and then sank weakly into a chair.

"Yes, I am your Uncle Mark," the man returned, a touch of bitterness in his tone; "but I scarcely expected that you would acknowledge me as such. Where is your father?"

"Dead."

Mark Alexander staggered as if some one had struck him a sudden blow.

"When did he—die?" he asked, with whitening lips.

"Six years ago last November."

The man sank back into his chair, and bowed his head upon the table, with a groan.

Profound silence reigned in the room for several minutes, while each occupant was tortured by bitter thoughts.

Virgie could scarcely realize that at last the man who had wrought her father's ruin was sitting in her presence. She had never seen him but once since that dreadful time when the thunderbolt had fallen to crush them all, and that had been when she had fled from him in the street more than three years previous. She wondered how he had found her now. She had hoped she should never meet him again; she feared him; she abhorred him for the crime and wrong he had committed.

Her heart was even now filled with great bitterness toward him, for, but for him her dear father might have been living, an honored and respected citizen of San Francisco, and she could only remember how he had suffered, how, believing his name forever dishonored, he had fled, as it were, into the wilderness, there to drag out a weary existence among strangers.

A heavy sigh at length aroused her from these unhappy musings, and she glanced at her companion.

She could see that he, too, was sadly changed.

Evidently the last twelve years had been far from happy ones with him. His bowed form, his haggard face and gray hair, all told of a mind ill at ease, of a heart tortured by fear, if not with remorse.

Apparently, too, he had been very ill; he might even be so still, for he was fearfully emaciated, his face was hueless, and he was trembling with either weakness, cold, or emotion, perhaps all three combined.

His coat was drenched in the heavy rain in which he had come, and he looked so utterly wretched and forlorn, that something of pity began to crowd the anger from her heart.

"Uncle Mark," she said, trying to steady her trembling voice, "you have taken me so by surprise that I am forgetful of my duty. Remove your wet coat, and come nearer the fire, while I ring for a cup of tea and some supper for you."

"Ah! then you will not turn me out again into the storm. Still you cannot have much but hatred for me in your heart," he returned, lifting to her a face that was almost convulsed.

"I trust that nothing would make me unmindful of the duties of hospitality, especially toward one who is ill and suffering as you appear to be," Virgie answered, as she arose and went out to confer a moment with Mina regarding the comfort of her unbidden guest.

"Where is Aunt Margaret?" she inquired, when she returned, a few moments later.

"Dead."

"Ah! and Philip?"

"Dead—and little Bertha, too. All are gone—victims of cholera, while I have not known a well day since I had it," the man answered, in a harsh, unnatural voice.

Virgie felt the tears rise to her eyes, and her heart softened still more. Surely his punishment had begun, and in no light manner, if death had so quickly robbed him of all his family, ruining his own health also.

"How did you know that I was here in San Francisco?" she asked, after another painful pause.

He started at her question.

"I saw you here more than three years ago. I was not quite sure it was you the first time I met you, and I followed you, hoping to learn where you lived; but you evaded me without knowing it, that time. The next day I haunted the place where I lost sight of you, and came upon you just as you turned the corner, you remember. You knew me, I was very sure, by the look of dismay that sprang to your eyes. I was more sure after your little strategy in that store. But I wanted to see you desperately, Virgie. Didn't you see my advertisement among the personals?"

"Yes; but I—could not meet you. I—could not forget," faltered Virgie.

The man shivered at her words.

"Well, I cannot blame you. But never mind that now. I meant to find you if I could; but I made up my mind after a while that you and Abbot had left San Francisco—I had not a thought that he was dead—and so I went elsewhere to hunt for you. I have spent the last three years in wandering about, but finally came back here to end my days. I was in at Knight's bookstore a day or two since. There was a pile of new books on the counter, and as I stood looking at one of them a gentleman came for one, and said to a boy, 'I want you to take one of Mrs. Alexander's new books around to her.' The name startled me. I turned to the title page, and saw 'Virginia Alexander' printed there, as the author. I bought a copy, and followed the boy here. I should have come to see you yesterday, but I was not able to get out; I had hardly strength sufficient to-day, but to-night despair drove me out in spite of the storm."

"I am afraid you were imprudent. But what can I do for you, Uncle Mark?" Virgie asked, hardly knowing what to say to the returned fugitive.

"I will tell you that by and by. Can I—will you let me stay here to-night?" he humbly asked.

Virgie had but two beds, her own and her servant's, but she had not the heart to send him forth again into the storm, he looked so ill and miserable; so she replied, with a look of pity:

"Yes, if you wish."

The poor creature broke down and sobbed at her kindness, but he recovered himself after a moment, and turned away from her gaze.

"It is my nerves," he explained; "I am a total wreck; I am utterly shattered."

Mina now came in with a tempting little supper, and he was more composed and cheerful after he had eaten something and taken a cup of tea, and soon began to talk more freely of his past.

He had been in the East Indies, he told Virgie, engaged in the spice trade, most of the time since his flight from San Francisco. But he had never known a moment of peace since the day that he had fled with all the available funds of the bank, of which he had been the cashier, and his brother the president, for he had known well enough that the good name of the latter would have to suffer as well as his own.

"At first," he said, "I tried traveling, throwing myself into every excitement, and took my family with me. But it would not do; the fortune which I had stolen and was trying to enjoy, was like a mill-stone about my neck; the word 'thief' was branded upon my heart with every beat of my pulse, until, in despair, I at last located at Batavia, on the island of Java, and threw myself, heart and brain, into business. I invested the most of my ill-gotten gains where they would be safe, and began to speculate with the rest. The Bible says that 'the wicked shall not prosper;' but I did—if you call it prospering to have money literally pouring in upon you and be nearly distracted with an accusing conscience at the same time. The richer I grew the more wretched I became. I had heard that your father had sacrificed all that he was worth toward wiping out my iniquity; but of course I knew that it could not begin to make my defalcation good, and that people would only scoff and sneer, and say it was all pretense—doubtless we were in league and would share equally in the spoils. I knew his high sense of honor, and how sensitive he was, and I believed the blow would crush him."

"It did! it did!" cried Virgie, bursting into a passion of tears, as all the sad past came pressing upon her with this recital.

"Poor child! poor child!" returned her uncle, tremulously. "But you and your father were in a state of bliss compared with me. Then there came that terrible epidemic sweeping all whom I loved in three days from the face of the earth, and bringing me, also, very near to death's door. When it was all over, and I knew that I was to live, I felt that there remained but one thing for me to do—to come back here and make an open confession of everything, and atone, as far as I was able, for the mischief I had wrought. If I could have found Abbot I should have done this long ago. Oh, my brother, I wish you had not died!"

Again he broke down, and Virgie felt herself fast melting toward him.

She could not but feel that his repentance had come far too late, but he was much too wretched not to appeal to her sympathies.

They talked for several hours, she telling him all that had occurred since his flight, though she touched but lightly upon her individual sorrows.

But he appeared so exhausted that she finally persuaded him to retire, giving up her own room to him, she and little Virgie occupying Mina's, while the girl slept upon a lounge in their small dining-room.

When morning came Mr. Alexander was too ill to rise, and feared that he was going to have a relapse of his former illness.

He grew better, however, toward evening, and seemed to be so grateful for the care which his niece had given him, so repentant for the sorrow that he had brought upon her, that she was deeply touched.

After a few days he appeared much stronger, and seemed greatly interested in Virgie, her work, and particularly in her little one. Still, he did not seem to be quite at his ease.

"I did not mean to be such a burden upon you, Virgie," he said, humbly, one afternoon, as she was performing some little service for him.

"I do not consider you a burden. I am glad if I can make you comfortable, Uncle Mark," she returned, kindly.

"You shall not be a loser for your kindness to me," he added, smiling.

Virgie turned upon him sharply, her face flushing crimson, her eyes blazing.

"Uncle Mark," she retorted, in a clear, decided voice, "whatever I have done for you has been done from sympathy, and because I felt it my duty to minister to your needs; but I shall never receive any compensation from you—I could not. If you are as rich as you have hinted several times, I want you to right the wrong that you committed so long ago. There is much that still remains unpaid, even though the bank has long since resumed business. Many depositors lost heavily; there were several years that no interest was paid to them, and their funds were so locked up that they could not have what rightfully belonged to them, and much suffering was occasioned by it. All this—*everything* must be paid to the uttermost farthing."

"It shall be done. I will do all that can be required of me. But, Virgie, *you* have been the heaviest loser of all through what your father paid out for me, and that will be one of the debts to be canceled with the rest. Don't let your pride prevent my relieving my conscience of that obligation," said the sick man, tremulously.

Virgie had not thought of the matter in that light before. Her chief desire had been to have a confession, and restitution made to the bank and all depositors, and thus clear her father from all imputation of wrong-doing. She had never reckoned herself among the number of the injured—never counted upon receiving a dollar in return for the sacrifice her father had made. To have his honor re-established, and then be able to bring his body back to rest beside her mother, would give her more joy than she ever expected to know again in this world.

"Papa's good name is more to me than all else," she said, tearfully.

"Dear child, it shall be fully restored; his honor vindicated. Oh, that he could have lived to know it! That it could not is the hardest part of my punishment. But after I have done that, you will not refuse to receive what I can offer you?" pleaded Mark Alexander, earnestly.

"Can you satisfy *all* claims upon the bank?" Virgie asked, in surprise, for she knew that the interest of all those years would amount to a great deal.

"I can do far more than that, and to-morrow I will make a beginning, if I have the strength. What I do must be done quickly, for my days are numbered."

CHAPTER II.
VIRGIE RECEIVES A MYSTERIOUS PACKAGE.

Virgie, remembering her promise to Mr. Knight, to let him know if she ever met her uncle in San Francisco again, determined to consult with him regarding Mark Alexander's intentions.

She knew that he would advise her rightly, and relieve her from all anxiety in the matter. She feared that her uncle might be arrested and tried for the crime that he had committed, in spite of the fact that he was willing and eager to make full restitution, and he was far too ill a man for any such excitement.

But she did not have to fear this long, for he was suddenly attacked with very alarming symptoms and his physician told him plainly that he would never leave his chamber again.

"It is far better so," he said to Virgie, when he told her of the verdict, "for nothing can occur now to cause you any annoyance. I shall be glad to have 'life's fitful fever over,' and can die content if you will assure me that you forgive me for all the unhappiness I have caused you."

"Yes, I do, Uncle Mark," she answered.

And she was sincere. She could freely forgive him for all *she* had suffered through his wrong-doing, but she could not quite forgive him for the shame and sorrow her father had endured on his account.

To be sure the truth would all come out now, restitution would be made, and the world would know that Mark Alexander alone had been guilty of the crime imputed to his brother as well; but her father was not there to experience the benefit of tardy justice, and, though grateful, she was only partially content.

She sent for Mr. Knight and confided the whole matter to him. He told her to leave it all with him, and he would see that full justice was done.

After a conference with the invalid a lawyer was sent for, a full confession of the crime was written out and signed in the presence of the required number of witnesses, after which he made his will, making Mr. Knight his executor, and bequeathing all that was necessary of his fortune to liquidate his indebtedness to the bank he had wronged, the remainder to go to his niece, Virginia Alexander, and her heirs forever.

After this important business was finished, the lawyer and witnesses gone, Mr. Alexander requested Virgie to bring him a package of papers she would find in the lower part of his trunk.

She complied, and then he asked her if she would assist him in looking them over, as he wished to destroy those that were of no value and leave some directions regarding the others.

There were a great many of them, and they were of various descriptions, therefore their examination required some time. But at last everything seemed to be arranged satisfactorily—all but one sealed package, which the invalid had laid aside from all the others.

This he now took up, remarking, as he viewed it thoughtfully:

"There is quite a romantic history connected with this, and it came into my hands in a remarkable way. I am going to tell you the story, and then give the package to you to keep for the owner, if you should ever be fortunate enough to find her."

"Ah! It is something that some one has lost?" Virgie remarked, looking interested.

"Yes. I stopped in London for a few days on my way home from the East. But on the last day of my stay I gave up my room at the hotel several hours before I left, and went into the gentlemen's reception-room to read my paper. I was far from well, and the noise and smoke there annoyed me exceedingly, so I stole into a small parlor devoted to ladies' use, and seating myself behind some draperies in a bay-window, gave myself up to the enjoyment of solitude and the news of the day. I must, however, have soon fallen asleep, for I was not conscious that any one had entered the room until I heard the voices of two ladies almost beside me. How long they had been there I do not know, and my first impulse was to make my presence known and then leave the room. But this seemed an awkward thing to do, particularly as they might have been talking some time before I awoke, and they might consider me very ill-bred for having remained a listener to what had already been said. Then, I thought, I was an utter stranger to them; I was about leaving for another country, and whatever the nature of their conversation, it could make no difference to either them or me, if I did overhear it. It proved to be very harmless, however, until just as they were about to separate, one lady remarked to the other:

"'By the way, as we are going to the Continent for a while, I want to ask you to take charge of a package for me. It would be valuable to no one excepting myself, and yet if it should chance to fall into other hands during my absence, it might occasion me a great deal of trouble. I know it will be safe with you, and if anything should happen to me while I am away, I want you to burn it.'

"'Very well, I will do as you wish,' returned her companion, as she appeared to receive something that the other handed to her.

"They conversed a few moments longer, and then arose and left the room. I judged that they had met there at the request of the lady who was going abroad, simply to take leave of each other, and I thought no more of the affair until I took my seat in the evening train for Edinburgh, whence I was to go to Glasgow to await the sailing of a steamer for home. A lady entered just after I was seated, and while giving some directions to the porter who brought in her luggage, her voice struck me as familiar. Still I could not place her—indeed I was very sure I had never seen her before, and being exceedingly wary I settled myself in a corner and was soon fast asleep. When I awoke it was very dark outside, though the coach lamps burned dimly above me, and I found myself alone in the compartment; my companion, whoever she might have been, had left the train.

"Judging from the cramped condition I was in, I must have slept a long time and very soundly. I arose to stretch myself and change my position, when my foot struck some object on the floor. I stooped and picked up the package. Taking it nearer to the light I found that its seal was stamped simply with a coat of arms, while there was written on the back of the wrapper, 'To be destroyed, unopened, in the event of my death.'

"Instantly it flashed upon me that the lady of the familiar voice, who had been my companion, was one of the women who had been in the ladies' parlor at the hotel that afternoon, and that this was the very package intrusted to her care by her friend. Of course I would not presume to open the package to ascertain to whom it belonged, and I had not the faintest idea what to do with it, for no names had been called during that interview to enlighten me as to the identity of the ladies.

"When the train stopped again I asked the guard at what station my companion had left. He did not know; he said the guards had been changed at Sheffield, and the lady must have got out before that, as I was alone in the compartment when he came on. I was both puzzled and annoyed. I did not like to intrust the package to any one connected with the train, for I judged from what the lady had said that it contained something of great importance—at least to her. I did not doubt that inquiries would be made for it, for doubtless the woman who had lost it would be in great anxiety about it. My time was not valuable, and I began to be considerably interested in my discovery, so I resolved to return to London, and wait to see if any inquiries were made regarding the lost package. Accordingly I took the next train back, and the following morning, I myself inserted a notice in some of the papers, describing what I had found and stating where it could be obtained. I remained in the city a fortnight, but no one ever came to claim the package, and though I closely examined the newspapers, no inquiry for it ever appeared. I felt that I had done my whole duty in the matter, so I again started for home, bringing my mysterious possession with me.

"It is just as I found it. I confess I have often felt a curiosity regarding its contents, but I have respected the owner's evident desire that it should remain a sealed matter to every one save herself. I am going to give it to you now, Virgie. Of course, I know it is very doubtful whether you will ever meet the owner, but I do not like to destroy it, fearing there may be something of importance contained in it. Here it is, just as I found it, and if you should ever happen to hear any one mention having lost a sealed package on the Edinburgh train, this may prove to be the one. It can easily be identified by the crest upon the seal."

Virgie took the mysterious thing and examined it with some curiosity.

It was of an oblong shape, nicely wrapped in thick white paper, sealed with red wax, upon which had been stamped a coat of arms.

"What a queer looking device," Virgie said. "A shield bearing a cross that is doubled crossed."

"Yet, it is what is called a patriarchal cross. I was curious about the crest, so I studied up a little on the subject of heraldry; and the motto is certainly an excellent one, '*Droit et Loyal*,' meaning 'Upright and Loyal,'" returned the sick man, with a sigh, as if the words were a stab at him.

Virgie turned the package over, and found written there, in an evidently disguised hand, the sentence, "To be destroyed unopened in the event of my death."

"I feel almost as if I hold the fate of someone in my hands," she said, a slight shiver disturbing her.

She was not naturally superstitious, but she experienced a very uncomfortable sensation in the possession of the mystic thing, and years after the words that she had just uttered returned to her mind with peculiar force; she did indeed hold the fate of a human being in her hands.

"If you do not like to keep it, if the knowledge of its possession becomes irksome or burdensome, then destroy it," her uncle said, as he noticed that she was strangely affected.

"I will keep it for the present," she answered. "There is no probability, however, that the owner and I will ever meet."

"I do not know; stranger things than that have happened, our lives cross those of others in a marvelous way sometimes," returned Mr. Alexander, dreamily. "I believe," he added, arousing himself after a few moments, "that some power stronger than myself has influenced me to preserve that package, and to confide it now to you. I am impressed that it may even prove useful to you. Let me advise you to take good care of it, Virgie, keep it, say for twenty years, if you should live so long, and then, if nothing has come of it, do what you like with it; by that time it is doubtful if it could do the owner either harm or good."

"Very well, I will do as you suggest, Uncle Mark," Virgie answered, and saying this, she arose and locked it in a small drawer in her writing-desk.

Mark Alexander failed very rapidly after that. Disease and remorse had done their work pretty effectually, and in less than three weeks from that stormy evening when he had come to Virgie he was laid to his last, long rest in Lone Mountain Cemetery.

After this Mr. Knight lost no time in carrying out the instructions he had received, and instituted measures for making ample restitution for the crime that had been committed nearly twelve years previous.

The bank from which Mark Alexander had stolen so largely had been nearly ruined. All payments had been suspended for years, and the most strenuous exertions were made to turn to the best advantage the comparatively small assets left, and thus prevent a total loss to the depositors and stockholders. It had been but a little while since it had been able to resume business upon its former basis, and it will be readily understood that the accession of nearly half a million dollars—the sum returned to them by the former criminal— was most joyfully received by the directors.

A statement of the fact was published, together with an announcement that all depositors who had suffered from the defalcation would receive remuneration for all loss and annoyance in the past.

Abbot Alexander, the former president, was exonerated from all blame. Every taint, every doubt and suspicion were removed from his name, and justice was at last rendered to an honest man. A glowing tribute was paid to his nobility of character, to his rare talents as a business man, and to the spirit of self-sacrifice he had manifested at the time of the trouble, in giving up all his own wealth.

It was a day long to be remembered by Virgie, when all this was proclaimed to the world. The papers were full of it, and seemed to vie with each other in trying to atone for the wrong which Abbot Alexander had so patiently suffered, which had broken the heart of his gentle wife and driven his wife and his beautiful daughter into exile. It was tardy justice, but it was ample and complete.

But little was said of Mark Alexander and his wonderful prosperity since his defalcation, but that little, while it did not conceal or condone the crime that he had committed, commended most highly that last act of his life.

It was also hinted in these same papers, that the talented author of "Gleanings from the Heights," and several other charming productions of the same character, was the daughter of the lamented bank president who had been so cruelly maligned.

"Oh, if my father could have but known of this!" Virgie exclaimed, when talking the matter over, afterward, with Mr. Knight.

"You may be very sure that he does know it," he responded, gravely. "It is to be regretted that he could not have known it before his death; it would have helped to soothe his last days. But still, if anything can add to his joy in another world, the fact that his name is to-day held up as one of the most honored in San Francisco, must contribute to it, as also must the knowledge that his daughter will henceforth be relieved from all pecuniary care or anxiety. You are really quite a wealthy young woman, my friend," the publisher concluded, smiling.

"Am I?" Virgie questioned, absently.

She was thinking of those weary years among the mountains when, day after day, her father came and went, to and from the mine, like a common laborer, toiling persistently and patiently, so that she might have a competence when he could care for her no longer. "And all for naught!" she mused, with a bitter pang, "for had not that also fallen into the hands of an adventurer?" It seemed to have been his fate to accumulate for others to spend.

"How indifferent you are! Have you no curiosity about the matter?" questioned Mr. Knight, archly.

"Yes, of course I have," Virgie answered, rousing herself from her reverie. "Is the amount that remains to me finally determined?"

"Yes; there will be about a hundred and fifty thousand dollars—not much more than half what your father sacrificed for his brother, but sufficient to make you quite independent."

"So much!" exclaimed Virgie, in surprise.

"It is quite a snug little fortune, and I am glad for you. There will be no longer any need for your working as you have done, and I am afraid I must lose my matchless designer."

"Indeed you will not," Virgie cried eagerly; "that is, if you will allow me to continue my work. I have become so accustomed to regular employment—I love my work so well, that I shall be far happier to continue it. I will not try to do quite so much," she added, thoughtfully, "now that there is no actual necessity for it; I will perhaps give you one or two designs a year, but I could not think of living an idle life."

"I shall be only too glad to get anything from your pen," Mr. Knight returned. "But what do you think about removing to New York? I am contemplating giving up my business here and establishing myself in New York city. My partner, who, as you know, is a younger man than I, wants to branch out a little more than I care to at my age, so I have sold out to him. Still, I, too, am unwilling to be idle, so I think I will go East and do a little quiet business on my own account."

"It matters very little to me where I am located," Virgie said, with a sigh. It was a little hard, she thought, not to have any ties anywhere. "I should like to travel a portion of every year, and I may as well make my headquarters in New York as anywhere."

And now it seemed as if a very peaceful, if not delightful future lay before her; yet, aside from the many advantages which her newly acquired wealth would enable her to give her child, its possession gave her but very little pleasure.

She did not believe that life would ever hold any special enjoyment for her again. Excepting her child, she had not a single object for which to live, nothing to look forward to. She cared little for society, indeed she shrank from meeting strangers; at least, those in her own position in life, although she went much among the poor, and spent money freely upon them.

When Mr. Knight went to New York she went also, making a quiet but elegant home for herself not far from his residence, where he and his sister kept bachelor's and old maid's hall, and there she lived her uneventful life, with nothing save a season of travel now and then, to vary its monotony.

Thus several years went by. She never heard one word either from or of Heathdale; she knew not whether Sir William was living or dead, prosperous or otherwise, though often her heart yearned for some tidings of him.

One summer, when little Virgie was nine years of age, they went for a week or two to Niagara Falls. Virgie had never visited the place, and she promised herself a rare treat in studying nature there in all its grandeur, and in making some sketches for the coming winter's work.

She reached the village late in the day, and was driven directly to one of the principal hotels, where she ordered a couple of rooms—for she had a maid with her—and then stepped to the office to register.

After she had done so she carelessly glanced over some of the preceding pages to see who were guests in the house.

At the top of one of the pages, and under the date of a week previous, she saw three names that sent every drop of blood back upon her heart and turned her giddy and faint.

"William Heath and wife. Master Willie Heath and maid," she read, and every letter seemed as if it had been branded in characters of fire upon her brain.

CHAPTER III.
VIRGIE SHALL YET HAVE HER INHERITANCE.

Could it be possible that the man who had been her husband had come again to this country, accompanied by the woman who had supplanted her?

They had a child too, it seemed, a young heir, and they were all underneath the same roof with her.

For a moment she was dazed with the knowledge; then she was tempted to dash the pen through her own name and fly to some other place.

But she did not like to make herself conspicuous; even now the clerk had noticed her emotion, and was asking her if she was faint and would like a glass of water. So she braced herself to face whatever might come, though she felt as if it would kill her to meet the man who had once called her wife.

She resolved to go to her rooms and remain in them, at least for a day or two, then she would quietly leave the hotel and go to some other.

She found her apartments very pleasant, overlooking the river and the rapids, while in the distance she could hear the never-ceasing roar of the falls. But there were no attractions in the place now for her; all interest had been swallowed up in the intense excitement that had taken possession of her.

She slept but little that night, and during all the next day she was wretched and almost ill. All her wrongs seemed to rise up afresh before her, and she wondered that Sir William had dared to cross the ocean lest her vengeance should overtake him. He was traveling, too, the same as he used to, as plain Mr. Heath. Oh, how supremely happy she had been in those lovely rooms in New York, when she had believed herself to be his honored wife, and was looking forward to a bright future as the mistress of Heathdale.

But now she believed another was reigning there. She wondered if she was fair and lovely; if she had ever suspected the wrong that her husband had done his first wife. She wondered, too, if Sir William had ever legalized that mock marriage after receiving the notice of his divorce from her.

All day she lay there, too miserable to rise, listening to every footfall that passed her door; she believed that she could recognize *his* step, even though a decade of years had passed since she had heard it.

When night came again she was nearly worn out, and, with little Virgie clasped close to her heart, she slept the sleep of exhaustion, and awoke the next morning feeling stronger and much refreshed, though still very unhappy.

She would not go down to breakfast, however, but had it served in her room. She had not courage to come face to face with the man who, she believed, had so wronged her; she shrank from him, but even more from the woman who, she supposed, occupied the position that belonged to her.

After breakfast she dressed her little daughter in the daintiest manner, and sent her out for a walk with her maid, telling the latter that she might keep Virgie out as long as desired, as she was not feeling well and wished to be quiet.

When they were gone she lay down again, and tried to think what was best for her to do. Should she go away immediately, and avoid all danger of being seen and recognized? Should she fly from the temptation that was fast laying hold of her to look once more upon the old-time lover—the father of her child?

She feared that it was not wise for her to linger there; indeed she knew that it would be far better for her peace of mind to turn resolutely away from all that pertained to the past, go elsewhere, and try to forget—if that were possible—that such a person as Sir William Heath had ever existed.

She fell asleep while musing thus, and was conscious of nothing more until someone knocked upon her door, and a childish voice called out:

"Mamma! mamma! oh, please let me in. I want to tell you something."

Virgie aroused herself, and going to the door, unlocked and opened it, and was confronted by her little daughter, her face flushed and eager, her hat hanging from her neck by its blue ribbons, her golden curls floating in charming disarray about her shoulders, while she held by the hand a bright, dark-eyed little boy, perhaps a year younger than herself.

"Oh, mamma!" cried little Virgie, all excitement, "I have had such a lovely time down stairs on the veranda. There was the nicest lady and gentleman there, and this is their little boy. We played a long time with some beautiful white stones, and we had some caramels and taffy, the lady told us some pretty stories, and Willie's papa sang us such a funny song; then they went away for a walk, and told Willie that he might come and play with me for a little while."

Something made Virgie grow very pale and still while her child was talking; something in those dark eyes of the little stranger, lifted in wonder and inquiry to her beautiful, white face, made her shrink and tremble, a terrible suspicion in her heart.

She stooped quickly and looked closer into the small, upturned face.

"Your name is Willie," she said, in a low, repressed tone—"Willie what?"

"Willie Heath," he answered, regarding her earnestly.

"Yes, mamma, and he lives away over the sea, in England—away over that water where poor papa went and——"

"Yes, dear," said Virgie, interrupting her, and though she had known well enough, the moment she saw him, who the child was, the sound of those two names smote her with such startling force that she reeled dizzily and was obliged to lay hold of the door for support.

"Poor mamma! your head is bad again, isn't it?" said her little girl, taking her hand and lifting it tenderly to her lips, while she looked pitifully into her white face.

"Yes, darling, and I shall have to lie down again; but you and your little friend may come in if you like," she forced herself to say, as she feebly made her way to a lounge, and almost fell upon it, a deadly faintness nearly overpowering her.

"No, mamma; we will go out into the hall and play," Virgie replied, while the young stranger regarded the stricken woman with wide, grave eyes. "I am going to get that box of toys that you bought me yesterday, then Willie and I will go away, and we will not make any noise, so you can sleep. Does your mamma ever have such dreadful headaches?" she asked of the boy.

"No, but papa does sometimes; then he has to stay in a dark room, and everybody has to keep as still as mice," he answered.

It seemed to the suffering woman as if she could not suppress a moan of agony to hear the child call that man "papa," and she wondered if he ever knew what it was to have such a heartache as she was at that moment suffering.

Little Virgie secured her box of playthings, and then the two children tiptoed out of the room, softly shutting the door after them, while Virgie lay another hour trying to compose herself and rally her shattered nerves.

She arose at last with the fixed determination to have one look at the man and woman whom she believed had ruined her life—just one glance to see how life had dealt with them, and then she would fly from all danger and temptation.

She arrayed herself in a lovely dress of black lace, made over rich lavender silk, and looped here and there with glistening ribbons of the same color. She had coiled her abundant hair in a coronet about her shapely head and pinned it with a golden arrow, in which there gleamed a single diamond. Her ornaments were of dead rough gold, fashioned in some quaint design, and she fastened in her belt a cluster of white acacia blossoms, which made a lovely contrast against the black and lavender of her dress.

She was exquisitely beautiful, and she realized the fact as she finished her toilet, and she could not help wondering what she—that other woman was like—the woman who had won her husband from her.

She could hear the merry voices of the children, who were still at their play in the hall, and a bitter smile curled her lips as she thought how unconscious they were of each other's identity, or of the torture she was suffering to have them thus together, two rivals, she believed, for the same name and inheritance.

After a little she went to her door and looked out at them. The children were both seated upon the floor, with Virgie's toys between them, and were chatting gayly with all the unconscious freedom of childhood.

"Oh, mamma, you are better!" cried Virgie, catching sight of her mother, her face lighting with pleasure, "and how nice you look! Willie," turning with an impressive air to her companion, "do you know I think *my* mamma is the prettiest mamma there is in the world; yours is very nice and grand, but I *don't* think she is quite as lovely as mine."

The boy fixed his eyes on Virgie, and looked gravely thoughtful for a moment, as if debating the point in his mind, and she was amused, in spite of her pain, by his evident desire to be guilty of no disloyalty, and yet not wound his new friend by contradicting her assertion, as he replied:

"Well, perhaps; but my *papa* is very handsome. Where is your papa?"

"Sh!" Virgie whispered, as her mother turned quickly away at the question and walked to the end of the corridor, where there was an alcove inclosed by rich draperies, "it makes mamma very sad to say anything about my papa. We lost him when I was a little baby."

"Lost him!"

"Yes; he went away over the same sea that you had to cross and he never came back."

"Oh! he was drownded!" whispered the little fellow, in an awe-stricken voice, and looking exceedingly shocked.

"What is your mamma's name?" he asked, after a pause.

"Virginia—the same as mine. What is yours?"

"Margaret, and it means 'a pearl.' Papa sometimes calls her his 'pearl of great price.'"

"Oh!" moaned Virgie from behind the draperies, as she caught these words, "a pearl of great price, indeed."

Just then a door midway of the corridor opened and another lady came slowly down the lofty hall.

She was tall and commanding in figure; not so slight or graceful as Virgie, but possessing a sweet and gracious dignity that was exceedingly pleasing.

She was a perfect blonde, and her beautiful golden hair was gathered into a massive and graceful knot at the back of her head. Her eyes were blue, her cheeks delicately tinted with pink, and a rare, winning smile played about her sweet mouth.

She was dressed all in white. A robe of some soft clinging material was *en traine*, very artistically draped and elaborately trimmed with a profusion of white satin ribbons. She wore an elegant set of opals surrounded with diamonds, and was truly a beautiful and distinguished looking woman.

Her face gleamed with infinite tenderness as she drew near the children.

"Why, are you still playing together?" she asked, as she stopped beside them; "you seem inclined to be very friendly."

"Yes, Virgie is a very nice girl to play with," returned Master Heath, with the air of one paying a great compliment; "and see what she has given me, mamma," he added, holding up a handful of toys.

"Do not let the little girl rob herself," said his mother, in a voice of tender caution.

"No; she made me take them; and—oh, mamma! I have seen her mamma—she was here just now—such a lovely lady! And Virgie says she lost her papa when she was a little baby—he was drownded."

"Drowned, you mean, Willie," corrected the lady; "how sad! but perhaps you ought not to talk about it, dear," she added tenderly, as she bent forward and softly stroked Virgie's glossy hair with her jeweled hand.

There were tears in her eyes as she said it, and though Virgie, in her hiding place behind the draperies, could not see these, she could hear the slight tremulousness in her tones, and she knew that she was a tender-hearted, sympathetic woman.

She then began to talk about something else and thus led their minds away from the sad topic until in a few moments they were laughing in the merriest manner—the childish voices ringing out fresh and clear, that of the beautiful woman like a silver bell.

Virgie saw and heard all with the keenest pain in her heart and though a torturing jealousy filled her soul—a sense of wrong and humiliation—from the belief that another had supplanted her in the heart and home of the man she loved, yet she could but own the worth, the beauty, and the fascination of that sweet, womanly woman who seemed so unconscious of wrong, whose heart was so full of tenderness and sympathy for the sorrows of others.

Oh, if, as she stood behind those curtains peering out upon that merry, attractive group, she could have known how very near she was just then to happiness and an explanation of all the dark past, she never would have concealed herself as she did. She would have made herself known; she would have sought rather than shunned that beautiful woman in white, and learned the mistake that had so embittered the last ten years of her life.

But she could more resolutely have faced a wild beast than those pure, innocent eyes and that happy smile. At first she had thought that she would go down to dinner, she would assert herself and make her presence a living reproach to the guilty pair.

But now she knew she could not; her strength would fail her, and she only longed for an opportunity to steal away unobserved to her room and hide her wretchedness once more from every human eye.

She turned away from that pretty tableau where her darling was so happy, and gazed out upon the street beneath her; but she saw nothing, heard nothing, for the tumult within her heart and brain.

She was conscious of nothing else till a movement almost beside her caused her to turn suddenly, and she found herself face to face with William Heath's wife.

"I beg your pardon," said the latter, flushing slightly as she met the startled, surprised look that shot into Virgie's eyes; "I did not know that any one was here. I came to find a book that I left here yesterday."

Virgie bowed, and moved aside to see if she was hiding it; but her heart beat almost suffocatingly, and she was as white as that cluster of acacias in her belt.

Yes, there was a volume lying on the chair beside her, which Mrs. Heath recognized, remarking as she took possession of it:

"Ah, yes, this is it. Thank you; I am sorry to have intruded upon you." Then, with an upward, admiring glance into the beautiful face, she added: "Pray, excuse me, but are not you the mother of the little girl who is playing with my son in the corridor? The resemblance between you is very striking."

"Yes, Virgie is my daughter," Virgie answered, laying an unconscious stress upon the pronoun.

"She is a dear little thing—so merry, yet so gentle and affectionate," remarked Mrs. Heath, with a tender inflection which somewhat softened her listener, "and I believe she is the loveliest child I ever saw. How old is she?"

"She was nine in June."

"And my boy is eight," smiled the fond mother, with a proud, backward glance; "and he seems to have become really attached to Virgie during the little time they have played together. Have you been in Niagara long, Mrs. Alexander?"

Virgie started at being thus addressed by the woman who bore the name which had once been rightly her own.

"We arrived the day before yesterday," she said, briefly.

"Ah! So recently?" replied her companion, wondering why the beautiful woman should be so reserved. "Then you have had no opportunity to see the attractions of the place, and it is wonderful here. I have never seen anything so grand in all Europe as these mighty falls and the rapids."

She was so sweet and gracious, and evidently so desirous of pleasing, that Virgie was seized with an impulse to show her the better side of her character. She felt sure that they would meet again some day when, perhaps, their relative positions might be reversed, and something like a feeling of pity for the lovely woman prompted her to put aside her pain, her jealousy and bitterness, and exert herself to be agreeable.

She responded cordially to the remarks she had just made relative to the scenery of that locality, and thus, once launched, she talked as she had never talked before—of nature, of art, of literature, of men, and things generally; and when, half an hour later, the two women separated, Mrs. Heath was fascinated, almost enraptured.

"I have never met any one so brilliant or beautiful before," she murmured to herself, as she went to call her boy from his play, remarking that he must bid his little friend "good-by, since papa had decided that they were to leave directly after dinner."

Several hours later, as the twilight had begun to deepen, Virgie, weak and pale from the excitement of the day, sat upon the balcony opening from her room, eagerly watching a little scene below.

A carriage had just been driven to the door. Two large trunks were brought out from the hotel and strapped upon it, then a gentleman and a lady with a little boy and maid followed.

Virgie crouched down behind the railing and strained her eyes for a look at that tall, manly figure, firmly believing it to be Sir William Heath—her recreant husband.

He stood by the carriage door and assisted his wife to enter with affectionate care, seeing that she was perfectly comfortable before he attended to anything else; then he caught his boy in his arms, and with some playful remark, which the eager ear above could not catch, tossed him lightly in beside his mother. Then the maid was kindly assisted, after which he entered himself, and the travelers were driven away.

But Virgie, with all her anxiety to do so, had not been able to catch even one glimpse of that face. There was something familiar about the form, although it was somewhat stouter than Sir William had been ten years ago, while he had spoken so low that she could not tell whether it was the old loved voice or not; but as the carriage was whirled away in the growing dusk she felt a hundred-fold more desolate than ever before.

They were so happy, she so miserable! Why, oh, why must such things be?

Then a different mood took possession of her, and she grew hard and stern.

"It is coming—a day of retribution will surely come," she said. "There may be a son to inherit the title, but, if he told me the truth, the eldest born inherits the bulk of the property, and Virgie shall yet have her inheritance."

CHAPTER IV.
A STARTLING DISCOVERY.

It was a great relief to Virgie to know that the Heaths were gone, for now she would be perfectly free from all restraint and could go about as much as she desired without the fear of encountering them.

She remained a fortnight at the falls, visiting every place of interest in the vicinity, and making many beautiful sketches. Then she turned her face westward and northward, following the great lakes, intending to see much of the scenery of Michigan and Wisconsin before her season of travel should end.

She traveled very leisurely, never hurrying from place to place, for she strove to get all the enjoyment possible out of her tours, both for herself and her little girl, who was never happier than when journeying in this easy way.

But once they were obliged to ride all night. It was not often that Virgie would allow herself to do this, for they could not rest well upon the cars, but in this instance it seemed to be necessary in order to make connections.

She retired early for the sake of little Virgie, who was nervous at being on the train at night, they taking the lower berth of their section, while the maid occupied the upper one.

Virgie was very weary and soon dropped asleep without a thought of danger or of the terrible tragedy that was so soon to send a score of those thoughtless travelers into eternity, maim as many more for life, and stamp every memory with a never-to-be-forgotten horror.

Virgie did not know how long she had slept, when she became conscious of several heavy thuds against the bottom of the car she was in, accompanied by violent jerks and wrenches, and a swaying from side to side; then it seemed as if they were being thrown into space; there was one awful moment of horror and suspense, then a terrible crash, mingled with shrieks, and groans, and prayers; after that darkness and oblivion.

When she came to herself again it was to find her little daughter clinging to her in an agony of terror, calling piteously to her to "wake up and take her out of that dreadful place."

She tried to sit up, but found that she could not, there was barely space between her own and the upper berth to admit of her moving at all. To make the situation even more appalling it was as dark as Erebus, while the cries for help and the shrieks of pain all around her filled her with a sickening horror, and she knew there had been a dreadful disaster.

"Are you hurt, darling?" she asked, an agony of dread at her heart, and her relief was almost as intense when the reply came:

"No, mamma, only so frightened by the dreadful noises."

Virgie had not removed her clothing, simply loosened it, and now it was the work of but a moment or two to gather her wraps about her, fold a shawl around Virgie and help her from the berth, though she found great difficulty in standing erect, for the car had been thrown partly upon its side.

She called to her maid; but there was no reply, and, fearing the worst for the poor girl, Virgie resolved to get her darling out of danger and then return to see what she could do for her unconscious servant.

They worked their way out of the car with difficulty, realizing as they did so that the portion where they had been was the least shattered of any—that they had been wonderfully preserved.

Virgie emerged from the debris as well as she could, and found herself in a swamp. She could now account for that sensation of being thrown into space, and the awful moment of suspense following before that terrible crash had come; the train had been pitched from its roadbed, she did not know how many feet above, and now lay a mass of ruins in a bog or meadow.

She bore Virgie to more solid ground, set her down by some bushes, and then, throwing her own mantle over her, bade her not move from that spot until she came back to her again.

"Oh! don't go back again, mamma," cried the child, clinging to her in terror.

"I must, darling," Virgie answered, firmly. "I cannot leave Mina to die there. Be a brave little girl and do not detain me. I will come back as soon as I can."

"But I am afraid, mamma."

"Nothing can harm you now, dear; we are both safe, thank God! while no one can tell how many have met their doom and are dead or dying."

She bent down and kissed the child tenderly, thankfully, and then sped back to the car, determined to know the fate of her maid.

All about her the direst confusion prevailed. Men were hurrying hither and thither. Women were weeping and moaning, and wandering about calling piteously for lost ones, while children were screaming with fright and pain.

It was lighter now, for two of the cars were burning, having taken fire from overturned lamps, and Virgie made her way more easily back into the sleeper she had left.

"Mina! Mina!" she called, springing toward the berth she occupied, and to her intense relief a muffled sound came back in reply, and she knew that she was not dead.

She found that the top of her car had been smashed in, and the girl, thus pinioned to her berth, was half-suffocated by the pressure from above.

Virgie never could tell afterward how she managed to release her, but by dint of encouragement and commands she succeeded in making the girl exert herself, and, using all her own strength, she by degrees got her to the edge of the berth and finally out of it.

"Are you badly hurt Mina?" she asked, as she supported the half-fainting girl, and wrapped a blanket around her trembling form.

"Yes, marm, my left arm is dreadful," the girl moaned, and Virgie could feel that it hung limp and helplessly by her side, and she knew it was broken.

"Well, we must hurry out of the car, for it is filling with smoke, and I fear has taken fire somewhere," she said.

They were just turning to leave the place when, from the very midst of the smoke there pealed forth a heartrending shriek:

"Help! help! Will no one save me?"

Virgie felt every nerve in her body creep at the sound.

"Oh, some poor creature is there, and will be burned to death if help does not come. What shall we do?" she cried.

Clearly Mina could do nothing with her broken arm, for she was moaning with every breath, and there was no one else at hand; every one who was able had deserted the car long since, and was either looking out for number one or assisting others elsewhere; but Virgie felt that she could not leave the sufferer, whoever it might be, to the terrible fate of being burned to death.

She helped Mina from the car, told her where she would find little Virgie, and then she flew back to find the origin of that pitiful cry for help.

"Where are you?" she called, as she groped her way toward the spot from whence it had seemed to proceed.

"Here. Oh! come quickly! I am almost suffocated! I shall be burned alive!" was the agonized response, accompanied by groans of pain.

It was a woman, Virgie knew by the tones, and all her sympathies were instantly aroused.

She found her at last, and her heart sank within her as she saw her condition, for the poor creature was wedged between a demolished berth and the side of the car in such a way that it seemed impossible to rescue her.

It was a sickening sight, for, already, Virgie could see little tongues of flame leaping up all about her and shooting out toward her as if eager for their prey, while the smoke was rapidly growing denser.

The woman saw it, too, and her face was almost convulsed with agony and fear.

"Oh, do help me," she prayed. "I shall be burned. I cannot die such a horrible death."

Virgie felt that she was powerless—she knew that she could not so much as stir that mass of debris.

"I will go and call some one," she said.

"No, no! You shall not leave me," screamed the woman, frantic with terror.

"Madam," Virgie returned, calmly but firmly, "it is impossible for me to do anything for you unaided. The best I can do will be to go for help; but first tell me who you are in case anything should happen to you before I can return."

"I am Lady Linton. I live in Hampshire County, England, and am just on a visit to this country with my son and daughter, and some other friends, who are now awaiting me in Chicago. Now go—go and save me if you can."

It would be difficult to portray with what stunning force these sentences fell upon the ears of Virginia Alexander.

Her heart almost ceased beating, while a thousand thoughts went flashing with lightning-like rapidity through her brain.

She had recently avoided a meeting as she supposed, with Sir William Heath; and had now encountered in this marvelous way his sister—the woman who had written those cruel letters to Mrs. Farnum so many years ago, but which were still stamped upon her brain so indelibly that she could repeat them word for word. This was the woman who had scorned her claims upon her brother—who had heartlessly advised her to "settle in some place where she was not known and try to bring up her child in a respectable way," who had insulted her by sending her a hundred pounds to soothe her disappointment for the loss of her husband and because she could not be recognized as the mistress of Heathdale; and now she lay crushed beneath a mass of ruins, doomed to a dreadful death unless the very woman she had so wronged and mocked should strain every effort to save her. It was truly a strange fate that placed her thus in the power of Virgie.

For an instant an evil spirit took possession of her heart and whispered:

"She helped to ruin my life; she mocked and scoffed at my misery, and she ought to suffer."

But the next moment she called out in clear, resolute tones:

"I will save you! have courage—do not fear," and she almost flew over the debris, through the gathering smoke and out of the car, where she seized a man by the arm and cried:

"Come with me; a woman is helplessly pinned down inside this car; it is on fire, and she will soon be burned to death."

She dragged him almost by main force into the burning wreck, and made her way back to the spot where she had left her suffering foe.

"I can never get her out of there—ten men couldn't do it before we should all perish," said her companion, when he saw her situation.

"You *must*! I tell you she *shall* be saved!" Virgie cried, almost savagely, and, seizing hold of one of the fallen timbers in her excitement, she gave it a wrench which told, and showed that it was not impossible as it had first appeared to rescue the unhappy victim.

Thus inspired and encouraged, the man braced himself and pulled with all his might at the berth in which the woman lay. It yielded; they knew they would save her.

A fearful shriek rent the air; then all was still.

"Oh! pull her out. I can brace this beam for a moment," Virgie cried, and calling all her strength and will to her aid, she did actually brace herself against one of those heavy timbers, holding it back, until the man dragged the unfortunate woman from her perilous situation, and then, gathering her all unconscious, in his arms, he staggered out of the now rapidly burning car, closely followed by Virgie, who had barely strength enough left to reach the open air.

"Lend a hand here, somebody," cried her companion, and three or four helpers sprang forward to relieve him of his burden, when he turned and caught the brave woman, who had risked her own life to save that of an enemy, just as her strength failed her and she would have fallen senseless, back into the burning wreck.

The account of her heroism flew from lip to lip, and many willing hands were stretched forth to minister to her. Restoratives were brought, a physician was called to attend her, and it was not many minutes before she rallied, although she was as weak as a little child from the terrible strain during those last few moments in the burning car.

But she refused all attention now.

"I do not suffer—I am uninjured; I am only temporarily exhausted. Go to those who need you," she said, and creeping to the spot where she had left her child, she gathered her close in her arms and burst into a passion of thankful tears—thankful, not only because they had been spared unharmed to each other, but because she had been enabled to obey the divine mandate "Do good unto them which hate you," and though Lady Linton might never know *who* had saved her—might never experience an atom of gratitude to her whom she had wronged, yet *she* would always have the blessed consciousness of evil resisted and a noble action performed.

CHAPTER V.
VIRGIE BECOMES A NURSE.

Three cars of that night train had been literally dashed in pieces, two more had been partially demolished, and only two baggage cars and the engine remained uninjured.

Twenty passengers had been killed outright, several were so badly injured that their death was only a question of time, and many were crippled for life.

It was a shocking casualty, and even those who escaped unhurt were so badly shaken up and so unnerved by the sight of the dead, the dying, and the sufferings of the wounded, that they dropped exhausted and almost helpless the moment the necessity for action was over, and all who could be removed had been taken out of the wreck.

The disaster had been caused by a broken rail on a bridge that spanned a small stream. The wrench and strain of the first car, as it was thrown from the track, had snapped the iron arch, the whole structure had then given away, and most of the train had been precipitated into the meadow below, with the fearful results already described.

The sleeper, in which Virgie had been traveling, was the least shattered of any, and most of the frightened passengers had escaped from it as soon as possible after it touched the ground.

One man affirmed that he went back afterward to ascertain if any one remained in the car, but there had been no response to his shout, he could see nothing, for all the lights had been extinguished, there had been no cries or groans, and believing that everybody had succeeded in getting out, he went elsewhere to render assistance.

It was supposed, and rightly, that Virgie, with her maid and child, and Lady Linton, must have been stunned by the shock of going over the embankment, and did not recover consciousness until all others had left the wreck, and thus, had it not been for the brave woman's energy and perseverance, they might have been left there to perish.

When she had recovered sufficiently to look after the comfort of her small family, she found poor Mina suffering extremely, her arm having been broken in two places, while she was otherwise badly bruised; and little Virgie, although she had escaped without even a scratch, had become almost frantic with terror on account of her mother's swoon.

There was a small village not far from the scene of the disaster, and to this the sufferers were borne, the kind-hearted people cheerfully throwing open their homes to them and offering whatever they had to make them comfortable, and their services also as nurses. Medical and surgical assistance was immediately summoned, and the whole place immediately became a veritable hospital.

Mina's needs were among the first to be attended to, and she bore the operation of having the broken bones set with much fortitude and patience.

After that was over she became comparatively comfortable, although Virgie hovered about her all day, ministering to her as tenderly as if she had been a sister, sparing neither her own strength nor expense to alleviate her sufferings.

But toward evening, when she had fallen into a heavy sleep, produced by an anodyne, and little Virgie, wearied out with excitement and the trying scenes that she had witnessed during the day, had begged to be put to bed, Virgie bethought herself of other sufferers and went out to ascertain if she could be of assistance elsewhere.

Her first inquiry was for Lady Linton, who, she found, had been carried to a neighboring cottage and was reported as very seriously injured.

She made her way thither, and was told that, although there were no bones broken, it was feared the lady had suffered some internal injury which might prove fatal.

She had been unconscious most of the day, but now she was lying in a heavy sleep that almost amounted to stupor.

Virgie asked the weary woman who told her this, if she could be of any assistance, and she replied that if she could come in and sit awhile with the sick lady it would give her a chance to get her husband's supper and put her house in order; she had neglected everything to attend to the sufferer.

Virgie willingly complied, and passing quietly into the sick-room, she sat down by the bed and looked upon her husband's sister, her heart filled with the strangest emotions.

She saw that she slightly resembled Sir William, although she was a good many years older and not nearly so attractive. This, however, might be owing somewhat to her injuries, for there were several bruises about her head and face; she looked haggard and worn; her hair was in disorder and thin and quite gray; one hand had been badly cut and lay bandaged upon a pillow beside her, and truly she was a pitiable object in her present condition.

For long years Virgie had entertained hard and bitter feelings toward this woman. She did not, of course, know the extent of the wrong of which she had been guilty, but she had never forgotten Lady Linton's arrogance, nor the scorn which she had expressed regarding her to Mrs. Farnum; still, as she now lay there before her, so helpless and miserable, she could feel only compassion and regret for her. Something of the divine nature always animates the heart and begets a certain tenderness for those whom we benefit, particularly if some signal sacrifice has been made to secure it.

She sat there beside the unconscious woman for an hour or more, changing the wet cloths on her bruised head and gently fanning her, for the room was far from airy or comfortable, although it was the best in the house.

Then the physician came in, and Virgie questioned him regarding Lady Linton's condition.

He could not tell just yet how serious her injuries were, he told her. They might not prove to be anything alarming, but her nervous system had undoubtedly suffered a severe shock which might prove to be worse than any hurt.

"Do you know her?" he asked, in conclusion, while his keen eyes searched Virgie's beautiful face curiously. He had heard something of the heroism which she had shown that morning in saving the woman's life.

"I know who she is," she replied. "Her name is Lady Linton."

"Hum! English, then," interrupted the doctor, with a quick glance at the figure on the bed. "Any friends in this country?"

"She mentioned that she was on her way to Chicago to meet her son and daughter, and some other friends, but I do not know their address."

"Where is her home?"

"With her brother, Sir William Heath, in Hampshire County, England."

Virgie flushed scarlet as she spoke this name which she had not uttered before in years.

"She ought to have some friends here to care for her, but he is so far away it would be useless to send for him, at least until we know more about her condition. Was she traveling entirely alone?"

"I judge so. She spoke of no one being with her when she was found."

"You found her; you saved her. I heard about it," said the doctor, his face glowing.

"I went for assistance," Virgie returned, quietly.

"You did much more than that, madam. Did you escape unhurt?"

"Entirely, and my little daughter also, for which I cannot be too grateful. My maid, however, has a broken arm, besides several bruises; but she is very comfortable, and requires but little attention, so if I can make myself useful by caring for any others who are suffering, I shall be more than glad to do so."

The physician thought a moment, and then asked:

"Have you ever had any experience in a sick-room?"

"Yes. My father was an invalid many months before his death."

"Then you might do good service here, if you are willing to devote yourself to this case under my direction. There's only one woman in the house. She cannot, of course, give her whole time to nursing, and this lady will need close watching and a great deal of attention during the next two or three days. Indeed she really needs someone who can be depended upon."

Virgie flushed again.

It was very strange, she thought, that she, of all persons, should be commissioned to care for Lady Linton at such a critical time.

But she did not hesitate; it was her duty to do what she could for her, without regard to her own personal feelings in the matter; her enemy was like the Levite who had been left wounded by the wayside, and it now fell to her to act the good Samaritan's part.

"Very well," she answered, quietly, "then you may consider that I am at your service."

The doctor looked relieved, and after giving her minute instructions for the night, he went his way to other patients, confident that he could not leave the sufferer in better hands.

As soon as the woman of the house was at liberty again, Virgie went back to see if Mina was comfortable, and to arrange for someone to wait upon her if she should need it during the night, and then she returned to her charge.

But there was very little change in Lady Linton's condition during the next two days. She slept most of the time, only rousing to take the nourishment that was almost forced upon her, and then sinking into that death-like stupor again.

But the third day she awoke and began to manifest some interest in her condition and surroundings, and seemed to remember all that had occurred.

Then, after a thorough examination, it was ascertained that her injuries was not nearly so serious as had at first been feared. There was a severe contusion on one side, where the broken timbers of the car had pinned her down to the floor; she had several ugly scratches and flesh wounds, besides bruises on the head, and one ankle was badly sprained. The stupor, as the physician thought, had been caused more by the shock to the whole nervous system than by her injuries, and he now said that if no new symptoms developed she would improve rapidly.

And it proved even so. At the end of a week she was able to be bolstered up in bed, and began to appear more like herself and to realize that she had another lease of life.

She had conceived a great liking for Virgie, although she had not been told, neither had she recognized the fact that she had saved her from death at the time of the accident. She treated her with the greatest deference—an unusual thing for the haughty woman under any circumstances—and expressed a great deal of gratitude for the attention she so freely bestowed upon her.

Once she had begged to be told her name, and Virgie had told her to call her "nurse." She shrank from telling her who she was lest she should recognize her.

"But you are not a nurse, you are a lady," she persisted, "and you are so kind to me I want to know you."

Virgie could not fail to feel a thrill of triumph at these words, she, who had been "that girl" and who had been held up to such scorn and contempt in those cruel letters so long ago.

"I am simply your nurse for the present," she replied, with averted face; "perhaps some other time before I leave you I will tell you my name," and her ladyship had to be content with that.

But Virgie did not remain quite so much with her after that, she did not need such constant care, and she left her more with the woman of the house. She went in several times every day, and was careful to see that she had every attention, but there was a quiet dignity and reserve about her which Lady Linton admired.

"Who is this beautiful woman who has been so kind to me—to whom I owe so much?" she asked the doctor one day.

"Truly she is a beautiful woman, and you do owe her a great deal. You owe her your life twice over," he answered, impressively.

"How so?" was the surprised query.

"In the first place she saved you from that burning wreck almost at the risk of her own life; in the second place she is the only one in the town who could be found to give you proper care; everybody else was engaged with the other sufferers, and during those days and nights when you lay in that heavy stupor, she never left you; she fed you, she ministered most faithfully to your every need, and brought you safely out of it."

"Was it she who came to me when I lay pinned down in my berth?" asked Lady Linton, gravely.

"Yes, madam."

"Who is she?"

"I am obliged to confess that I do not know her name," the doctor admitted, smiling. "I doubt if she knows mine either. We have not stopped to exchange cards in this business; it has been of too serious a nature to admit of much ceremony. I call her 'madam,' and she has, naturally, addressed me as 'doctor.'"

"She seems a thorough lady," said his patient, thoughtfully.

She had, as Sir William once told her she would, changed her ideas somewhat regarding American people since coming to this country.

"You are right, madam," replied the physician, emphatically. "It has never been my privilege to meet a more cultured lady nor a truer woman. I shall certainly ask her to favor me with her name and address before she leaves."

"Is she going away?" demanded Lady Linton, quickly.

"Yes; in a day or two, I believe; her maid is doing nicely now and able to travel. But, bless me, I must not sit chattering here when there are more than forty patients waiting for me."

And the brisk little doctor trotted off, leaving Lady Linton looking very thoughtful, and wondering who her mysterious but beautiful nurse might be.

CHAPTER VI.
"I AM THE WOMAN YOUR BROTHER LOVED."

The morning after the foregoing conversation between Lady Linton and her physician, Virgie went in to see the invalid, taking her daughter with her.

She had come to take leave of her ladyship, for they were going away to some quiet resort for a few weeks, for Mina's sake, and after that home to New York. She brought Virgie as a sort of shield from embarrassment, for she dreaded any effusions of gratitude from the woman who, she felt sure, would hate her even now, in spite of all she had done for her, for having won her brother's love; while, too, she had a curiosity to see if she would be attracted toward her child; she was a believer in the old adage that "blood is thicker than water."

The invalid's face lighted the moment the door opened to admit her kind attendant.

"I am so glad to see you," she cried, heartily; then her glance fell upon the beautiful child, and she added, with evident delight: "And you have brought your little daughter with you! Come here, dear, and let me see if you are as lovely as your mamma."

She held out both hands to her and the little one went composedly forward and stood before her, her dark eyes searching the woman's face with a look that thrilled her strangely, while she was deeply impressed with her wonderful beauty.

"You are very like your mamma," said Lady Linton, smiling down upon the sweet child; "all excepting your eyes. I rather imagine that those came from papa. What is your name, dear?"

"Virgie."

Her ladyship started slightly and glanced quickly at the child's mother, and something that she saw in that beautiful countenance made her grow suddenly pale.

Her mind went back to that morning when her brother had laid before her several photographs of his lovely wife, and she was almost sure—even though she had never looked upon them since—that there was a resemblance between that face and this; and the child's name was the same, too.

But no; it could not be; and she banished the suspicion from her as quickly as it came. It was only a "singular coincidence," she told herself.

"Virgie," she repeated, trying, but in vain, to resume her light tone, "I suppose that stands for Virginia. Well, my little maiden, do you know how kind your mother has been to me while I have been so ill?"

"Mamma is always kind to everybody," was the grave response, and Virgie wondered to see her in this strange, self-contained mood. She was usually very free and confiding with every one.

"What a loyal-hearted little girl!" laughed Lady Linton; "how thankful I am that you were spared for her and she to you from that dreadful accident. Your papa, too, must be a very happy man to know that both his treasures are safe."

"I haven't any papa." said Virgie, with a soft little sigh.

A painful thrill shot through Lady Linton's nerves at this, and she darted another look at the child's mother.

It was very strange! She wore no widow's weeds, she was not even in black! Instead, she was looking very lovely in her stylish traveling suit of dark gray, with a knot of pale blue ribbon at her throat and another in her hat.

"Yes, indeed," the mother interrupted, not liking to have the child questioned further, "we are very grateful for having escaped such danger. We came to tell you that we are going away to-day, though I would gladly remain, if I could be of use to anyone, and duty did not call me elsewhere."

"To-day!" exclaimed Lady Linton, in surprise. "I shall be very sorry to part with you," and her under lip quivered, for at that instant she thought of the debt she owed the beautiful woman.

Virgie bowed. She was laboring under a fearful constraint. She would gladly have avoided this last interview, but something that impelled her to come, if for nothing more than to let her ladyship see her brother's child, even though she was unconscious of the relationship existing between them.

"Is your maid doing well?" Lady Linton inquired, after a somewhat awkward pause.

"Thanks; yes, much better than I had hoped she would. She feels quite able to travel, is rather homesick, and longs to get away from this dreary place."

"It is a lonely place. I, too, shall be glad to rejoin my friends. I expect someone will come to me to-morrow, and the physician thinks that by the end of another week, I may also be able to get away. Oh, must you go?" the invalid concluded, regretfully, as Virgie arose to leave.

"Yes, my carriage will come for us in half an hour," she replied, glancing at her watch. "I am glad to leave you so comfortable, and I trust nothing will occur to retard your full recovery—that your visit to this country may not be spoiled by this accident."

Lady Linton looked up astonished, as these cold, measured words fell upon her ears.

Virgie had not meant to speak so frigidly, but her ladyship's reference to her "friends" made her surmise instantly that she was speaking of her brother and his family, whom she believed she had seen at Niagara, and it was with the greatest difficulty that she could control herself at all.

"Surely you are not going to leave me thus?" said the sick woman, reproachfully, "without even allowing me to clasp your hand; you, who have done so much for me, who have twice saved my life. Come here and let me kiss you good-by—let me tell you that I shall never cease to think of you with gratitude and love. Why, you have never yet told me your name! You must not go without telling me who you are, so that I can inform my brother and friends who was my deliverer from a dreadful death—who was my kind nurse during my critical illness."

Virgie was as pale as a marble statue now; she could bear no more, and she resolved that she would tell her the truth. She should tell her brother, any anyone else she chose, who had saved her, if she wished to do so.

"Run away, Virgie, and help Mina to get ready," she said to her daughter, "and I will come presently;" then, as the child obeyed, she turned back, and stood tall and straight before the woman who had wronged her.

"Lady Linton," she began, in low, intense tones that smote her like a whip, and made her shiver with dread at what might follow, "it is true, I suppose, that I saved your life at the time of the disaster: it is true, also, that I have tried to make you comfortable during your illness; but I have not done it to win your gratitude or to oppress you with any sense of obligation. I did it, first, from a sense of duty, as I would have performed the same service for any stranger in trouble; and, second, because I would not allow myself to turn coldly from you in the hour of danger and distress, because of a feeling of enmity toward you——"

"Enmity?" interrupted her listener, with pale lips, and putting out her hand as if to ward off a blow.

"Yes, enmity, for my heart was full of it when you told me who you were. If I had listened to the evil that surged through my brain on that dreadful night, if I had yielded to a spirit of revenge for past injuries, I should have turned my back upon you when you called upon me to save you, telling myself that you deserved no better fate. But I believe I am a Christian, a disciple of One who commanded us to 'love our enemies, to do good to those who despitefully use us,' and I wished to conquer that enmity, to subdue myself, to return good for evil; and that is why I tried to save you then, and afterward served you as tenderly as I would have served my own mother."

"Why—why! what are you saying? I do not understand," incoherently cried the startled woman, as she gazed wildly into that beautiful face before her, and began to realize something of the terrible truth yet to come.

"I did not mean that you should understand," Virgie resumed, speaking more gravely. "I did not mean that you should ever know to whom you owed your life. I meant to do what good I could for you, and then go quietly away, taking with me as my only reward, the consciousness of a duty faithfully performed. I do not know why I have spoken thus even now, but the words seemed forced from me by a power beyond my control. Perhaps it is because you asked me to kiss you, to clasp your hand in friendly farewell, when I was conscious that you would wish me to do neither, if you knew who I am, that you would shrink from me, repel me, perhaps even hate me more than you have ever done. I see that you begin to realize who I am. Yes. I am Virginia Alexander, the woman whom your brother once loved, for I believe even now that he did love me then—and who worshiped him, who would have devoted her life to his happiness, and considered herself blessed in so doing."

Lady Linton had fallen back upon her pillow as Virgie uttered that well remembered name, and now lay, as if transfixed, gazing upon her with a look of amazement mingled with something of terror.

A suspicion of the truth began to dawn upon her when the child had told her name; it had been strengthened when she had so innocently said she had no papa, and it was now confirmed by Virgie's open declaration.

The knowledge almost paralyzed her; she could neither move nor speak; she had no power but to stare with a helpless, appalled look at that perfect figure, that pale, beautiful, high-bred face, as she realized, at last, the enormity of the wrong of which she had been guilty.

"You have seen my little daughter," Virgie resumed, after a moment, with a tender, even pathetic inflection; "she is also your brother's child, and the heiress of Heathdale——

"Does that offend you?" she asked, as Lady Linton shrank again, as if from a blow, at these words. "It is to be regretted, but it is a fact which nothing can change, and she will one day claim her own, even though her mother is no longer the wife of her father, and I trust that she will then do honor to the name and position which she will assume. You may rest assured that I shall attend most faithfully to her education, for it has been, and still shall be, my chief object in life to make her worthy in every way to be received as a representative of the 'ancient and honored house of Heath.' Pardon me if I seem ironical," Virgie interposed, a slight smile flitting over her lips as she quoted this sentence, which had been burned into her brain so long ago; "but I cannot forget the cruel things which you wrote to your friend, Mrs. Farnum, ten years ago. Do you blame me for refusing to clasp, in pretended friendship, the hand that penned them? or for shrinking from the kisses of one who so scorned and mocked me; who offered me money, as if my honor was a thing to be bought, my wretchedness and despair something to be alleviated with gold? You wrote of me is 'that person'—'that girl,' as if I belonged to a lower order of humanity; but, madam, my grandmother was an English woman like yourself, and perchance—though I assume nothing of the kind—there is as good blood in my veins as in your own. But," with a weary sigh, "perhaps I am wrong to recriminate thus. I had no intention of saying aught like this when I came to you. I am afraid I have been inconsiderate of your weakness, but my words have come unbidden. I wish you no ill. I think I have proved that during the past week. I wish your brother no ill, if he is happy in his present relation; far be it from me to wish him to suffer as I have suffered, although he has done me the greatest wrong it is possible for a man to do a woman. It is a strange freak of fate, Lady Linton, this meeting between you and me, and yet I believe I do not regret that we have seen and known each other; it has served to show you what the woman, whom your brother wooed and won, is like; that although she may not have belonged to the titled aristocracy of a kingdom, she was at least a true-hearted daughter of a grand republic, and in no way his inferior in character or intellect. We may never meet again, and we may; I cannot tell; but some day the wrong that has been done me will be righted through the justice which must and shall be rendered to my daughter."

As she ceased Virgie bowed gravely and then turned and quietly left the room, leaving Lady Linton more astonished and browbeaten—though it had been done in the most courteous and dignified way imaginable—than she had ever been before. For several minutes she sat staring, in a dazed way, at the door which had been so softly shut upon that graceful, retreating form, and almost feeling as if the whole interview must have been some hallucination of the brain.

That lovely woman—proud, beautiful, cultivated—with that magnificent form and carriage, the "low-born girl!" whom she supposed her brother had married! It seemed impossible! She was so entirely different from what she had conceived her to be.

Why, this brilliant creature was fitted to grace a throne—to shine a star in the highest circles of even her own country, of which she was so arrogantly proud, and she, by her cunning plotting, her falsehood and calumny, had debarred her from her home, from all the rights which legally belonged to her; she had brought shame and dishonor upon her, broken her heart, and, in so doing, had made her own brother's home desolate, his life almost a barren waste.

That beautiful child, too—that dainty, graceful, golden-haired fairy, with her mother's delicate features and her father's eyes; yes, they were strikingly like Sir William's own—she had tried to cheat her out of her heritage, and thus the grand old house at Heathdale was childless and was likely to remain so until this brave, determined woman came to demand justice, and to claim for her daughter the respect and honor that had been denied her as a wife.

She knew that she would do it if she lived; those quiet, resolute tones still rang in her ears, and she fell back upon her pillows weak and faint, heart-sick and terrified, and, for the moment, filled with remorse for the sin of the past.

She fully realized at last the enormity of her treachery and wickedness—the hardness of her heart, the selfishness of her nature.

She had been utterly heartless when she had attempted to crush the lovely girl whom her brother had won, and now the basely wronged woman had turned and heaped coals of fire upon her head. She had nobly put aside all sense of injury, and, knowing full well that she was serving an enemy, had saved her life and then given her kindest attention and tenderest care during her illness.

Lady Linton knew that she should carry a burdened heart to her grave on account of it.

Fired with sudden impulse, she started up and sharply rang her bell.

The woman of the house came to her almost immediately.

"Where is she?" demanded the invalid, wildly.

"Who?" asked her attendant, surprised by her excessive agitation.

"The lady who has been so kind to me. Call her back! Call her at once!"

"She has gone. The carriage has just driven away from the cottage where she stopped."

Lady Linton sank back again with a groan.

She was too late. She had meant to do a good deed. Under the impulse of the moment, and with a feeling of gratitude animating her, overcome with admiration for a rarely beautiful woman, and a sense of superiority; with the vision of that lovely, dark-eyed child still before her, she had resolved to make a full confession of all her wrong-doing, try to effect a reconciliation between those two who, she knew, still devotedly loved each other, and thus atone, as far as was possible, for the sin she had committed.

But the opportunity was gone, and when she came to think of it more calmly afterward, she began to upbraid herself for her momentary weakness, and to be glad that she had not committed herself.

Her good angel fled, her better nature was overcome, and she grew harder, more bitter than before.

"There will be some way out of it," she muttered, as she recalled Virgie's threat to claim her child's heritage. "I will fight it out to the bitter end. I am glad I did not make a fool of myself."

CHAPTER VII.
AFTER EIGHT YEARS.

Eight years have passed since Lady Linton, with her son and daughter, her cousin William Heath, and his family, visited America; since she so nearly fell a victim to that railway disaster, and was rescued by a woman whom she had hated, whom she now hated a hundred-fold.

It is a beautiful winter morning, and in the sunny, elegantly appointed dining-room at Heathdale an interesting group of five persons is gathered around the bountifully spread breakfast table.

At one end sits Sir William Heath, a handsome, dignified gentleman a little above forty, yet hardly looking that, for the fleeting years have touched him but lightly, in spite of the great sorrow which has lain so heavily upon his heart and robbed his life and his home of its chief joys—the love and presence of a fond, true wife, the patter of little feet, and the happy laughter and merry chatter of childish voices.

Opposite him, and engaged in serving coffee, is his sister, Lady Linton, who has changed greatly during the last eight years. She has grown old and wrinkled, and her face has hardened, if that could be possible. There is a cynical expression about her thin mouth, and her eyes are cold and critical in their expression, excepting when they rest upon her children, who now sit beside her, one at her right, the other at her left hand.

Percy Linton had done credit to the promise of his youth, and is a fine young man of twenty-one, honest, noble, and thoughtful beyond his years. He is lately home from Oxford, where he achieved great honors, and is now planning to return to the neglected and impoverished estate which has father's prodigality nearly ruined, with the intention of reclaiming it and restoring it to something of the thrift and prosperity for which it was noted under the care of his grandfather, for whom he is named, and whose mantle seems to have fallen upon him.

His mother is not at all in sympathy with these plans. She wishes her son to adopt a public career. She still has strong hopes that he will fall heir to her brother's title and property, in which case there would be no need of his spending the best years of his life in striving to redeem a heavily-mortgaged estate.

Sir William, however, heartily approves of his noble resolve, and promises to assist him in every possible way, and, with this encouragement, he has decided to devote himself to Linton Grange.

Lillian Linton is a brilliant and beautiful girl of nineteen. She is a clear brunette, with a lovely bloom on her cheeks, vividly red lips, dark eyes and hair. Her features are delicate and regular; she is tall and finely formed, attractive in manner, but in disposition and temperament she is much like her mother.

The remaining individual of the group was Rupert Hamilton, Sir William Heath's ward, and the child of his dear friend, Major Hamilton, who died several years ago. He is now a young man of twenty, tall and stalwart in form, with a well-shaped head set proudly upon a pair of square, broad shoulders. He has a handsome and intelligent face, with a pair of full, wine-brown eyes, which always meet yours with a clear, steady gaze, that proclaims a noble character and a clear conscience.

His nose is something after the Roman type, his mouth firm and strong, yet when he smiles, as sweet and expressive as a woman's. One would know at a glance that he was true and generous, kind and genial.

One could perceive also that Sir William loved him like a son by the affectionate glances which he bent upon him, by his answering smile whenever their eyes met, and the confidential tone which he used when addressing him.

The young heir to half a million pounds thought his guardian the noblest man in the world, and he would have deemed no service too difficult or disagreeable to perform for him.

He knew something of the trouble of his early life, that he had been married and parted from his wife, although he had never heard her name spoken, or asked a single question upon the subject, and he had always felt a peculiar tenderness and sympathy for him on this account.

The fact of Sir William's marriage was no longer a secret, although Lady Linton had tried every way to conceal it. It was not very generally known, however, even now; but in his own household and among his intimate friends it was understood that he had married a beautiful woman while on his first visit to America, and that some cruel misunderstanding had resulted in a separation. He had insisted upon this explanation, for hope was not yet quite dead in his heart that some time he might find Virgie, effect a reconciliation, and bring her home to Heathdale.

Those who knew that he was free to marry again, if he chose, sometimes urged him to do so and not allow his name to become extinct.

But he always replied, with a heavy sigh:

"I have a wife already, and some time, please Heaven, I shall find her. No other shall ever be mistress of Heathdale while I live."

This reply never failed to arouse the fiercest anger in Lady Linton, who grew more bitter with every year toward the woman whom she had wronged, and who had repaid her injuries with such kindness and Christian charity to her everlasting shame and humiliation.

"'Wife,' indeed!" she once retorted. "A woman who divorced herself from you in the way she did, coolly severing the bonds, which you seem still to hold in such reverence, is not worthy the name."

"But I loved her, Miriam—I love her still; I shall be true to her till I die," her brother answered. "Our separation has been the strangest thing in the world—it is wholly incomprehensible to me; but if I ever find we have been the victims of treachery, let the enemy who has meddled beware!"

Twice during these last eight years he had crossed the Atlantic and renewed his search for Virgie, but without obtaining the least clew of her whereabouts, and so he returned again to his home.

He never intruded his sorrow upon any one; indeed his life flowed along so calmly and smoothly that a stranger might have supposed that he had remained single from choice, although there was a wistful sadness in his eyes that impressed every one.

Of late he had interested himself considerably in politics and been in Parliament, having been returned for his borough several times.

But to return to the breakfast table, from which we have roved, and where an animated discussion was in progress, together with the disposition of the many tempting viands.

"I am sure I do not know what I am going to do without you during the next six months, Rupert," Sir William remarked. "Here I was anticipating having you all to myself for awhile, after you got through school, and now you want to go roving the first thing."

"Yes, I do want to see a little of the world I live in, I confess, before I choose my profession; and you have told me so many interesting things about America, and American people, that I have a curiosity to see the country and mingle with the people myself. Why can't you come with me, Uncle Will? then we need not be separated," concluded the young man, wishfully.

"I should be glad to, my boy, but my time and attention will have to be given to the interests of the borough for this year," responded his guardian. "The troubles in Ireland, too, bid fair to be pretty serious, and every true-hearted Englishman ought to give careful thought to the questions that are arising in connection with them."

"I hope that I am a true-hearted Englishman, but since I cannot cast my vote until next year, I presume you will not consider me disloyal for running away for a little while," Rupert said, earnestly.

"No, indeed, I want you to go, since you desire it so much, and, considering all things, this is the best time for you to go. Let me see; it is a Raymond excursion to California that you have decided to join after reaching New York, I believe."

"Yes, the circular which Raymond has issued is so attractive I could not resist it. I feel sure that by joining this party I shall see more of the country, in less time and to better advantage, than I could to travel by myself and lay out my own route."

"Will you be with a large party, Rupert?" Lillian asked, her color deepening and a rather anxious expression in her eyes.

Lillian Linton had learned to love Rupert Hamilton with a strong and passionate affection, and this attachment had been most unwisely fostered by her mother, who was still determined that her idolized daughter should marry her brother's wealthy young ward, and the heir to still greater prosperity and honor, if it was possible to accomplish it.

"I do not know how large the party will be, Lillian; probably there will be quite a number in it," he answered.

"All gentlemen?"

"Oh, no, I judge not from some hints that are given regarding the equipments necessary for the journey; for articles which only ladies require are mentioned in them."

Lillian lost some of her brilliant color, and her eyes drooped at this reply.

"But do you like the idea of mingling so freely with strange people?" she asked, with a slight curl of her red lips. "Americans too," she added, slightingly.

"Why, Lillian, are you so prejudiced against our neighbors over the sea?" exclaimed the young man, in surprise.

The girl shrugged her graceful shoulders and arched her pretty brows, but deigned no reply. The act, however, expressed far better than words could have done her contempt for the people of whom they had been speaking.

Percy glanced up at her with a roguish twinkle in his eyes.

"Rupert will doubtless meet some fair damsel among his party whose bright eyes and charming smiles will prove too much for his susceptible nature, and, before we know it, our loyal Englishman will have forsworn his colors and joined the great republic," he said, to tantalize his sister.

"Oh, Percy, how little faith you have in me," laughed Rupert. "Of course I expect there will be some fair damsels in my party, but doubtless they will be so closely guarded by jealous parents and vigilant chaperons that no young man of my age will have an opportunity to play the agreeable to them."

Neither of the young men observed the spasm of pain that contracted Sir William's brow at these remarks, nor the hardening of Lady Linton's face, as they thought of that episode in the life of the former, some eighteen years previous, while he was traveling in America.

"I trust that Rupert will not be beguiled into any discretions, no matter how attractive the ladies of his party may be; he owes it to his self-respect to choose his wife from his own countrywomen," remarked her ladyship, with a swift glance at her daughter, whose eyes were fixed upon her plate, as if she had no interest in anything but the morsel that she was diligently reducing to mince-meat with her knife.

"Are the ladies of America more artful in that respect than those of any other nationality, Lady Linton?" asked the young man, innocently, but with a quizzical smile.

"I am happy to say that I know but very little about them, but what I do know has not served to prepossess me in their favor," was the sharp retort of her ladyship.

"Miriam, I will trouble you for another cup of coffee," said Sir William, quietly, but in a tone which warned his sister that she had better not pursue the conversation further on that line.

Then he turned to his nephew, with a genial smile, saying:

"I only wish Percy had not been in quite such a hurry to settle at the Grange; I would really like to have you run over to the United States with Rupert for a little holiday before you begin work."

"Thank you, Uncle Will; but, truly, I feel that it would not be right to take either the time or the money for such a journey. My duty plainly points to the earliest possible restoration of my fallen house," the young man answered, gravely.

"I wish that every young man possessed as conscientious a regard for duty as you do, Percy. I confess I honor you for your desire to clear the Grange of all incumbrance, though I would gladly be your banker if you would consent to accompany Rupert."

"You have already been my banker to such an extent that I do not feel willing to draw upon you any more. I am very grateful for all your kindness, Uncle Will, but indeed my self-respect demands that I should begin to depend upon my own exertions; so I shall wed myself to the home of my ancestors until every debt is paid and the glory of the days of my grandfather is restored," Percy concluded, smilingly, but with a firmness which plainly told that his mind was made up regarding the course he was to pursue.

"I consider it a senseless, quixotic notion; I think you had much better sell the place and realize what you can from it, rather than spend the best of your life in trying to pay debts that other people have contracted," said his mother, resentfully.

"Sell Linton Grange," exclaimed the young man, aghast. "Why, mother, where is your loyalty to the home of more than a dozen generations?"

"I have suffered too much at Linton Grange to feel very much loyalty for bundles of mortgages, promissory notes, etc.," retorted Lady Linton, a deep flush suffusing her face.

"Percy is right, Miriam, so do not try to discourage him. It would, indeed, be a pity to sacrifice such a grand old place, while there was the least hope of reclaiming it. It will, no doubt, be up-hill work for the first few years, but, with the spirit which animates him, I am sure he will succeed, and his reward will be sweet," Sir William said, heartily, as he arose from the table. Then turning to his nephew, he continued: "I will ride over to the Grange with you in a couple of hours, and we will consider further the measures you proposed to me yesterday."

CHAPTER VIII.
A GLIMPSE AT LILLIAN LINTON'S HEART.

"Rupert, have you seen my orchids since they bloomed?" Lillian asked of her uncle's ward, as the family were leaving the dining-room.

"No. Are you indulging in orchids, Lillian?"

"Yes; I am wild over them. Uncle Will gave me several varieties on my last birthday, and they are just doing their best for me now. Come into the conservatory and let me show them to you."

"All right. I have a fancy for the pretty things, too," replied the young man as he followed the fair girl toward the hot-house, and thinking, as he did so, how lovely and graceful the girl was in her perfectly fitting morning robe of garnet cashmere trimmed with swansdown, and which harmonized delightfully with her brilliant complexion.

She took him to a sunny corner of the conservatory which Sir William had set apart and fitted up expressly to gratify this extravagant whim of his pretty niece, and where the young lady had really displayed much taste and appreciation of the rare things in which she was interested, both as to choice and arrangement.

They spent half an hour or more in examining the beautiful things, and Rupert became almost as enthusiastic as Lillian herself over them.

But she had no notion of allowing even her favorite flowers to monopolize all his attention. She had had a far more important object in view in bringing him there with her.

"So you are really determined on taking this American trip, Rupert?" she remarked, as they paused before a lovely arethusa in full bloom, from which she broke its fairest blossom, and, bending forward, fastened it to the lapel of his coat.

"Oh, Lillian, what a pity to break the pretty thing!" he said, regretfully.

"Not for you," she answered, looking up at him with a smile, and flushing as she met those frank brown eyes that were regarding her with unmistakable admiration. "You would be welcome to more if you wished."

"You are very generous," he returned, regarding the flower thoughtfully, and wondering what made her blush so when with him. "But about my trip. Yes, I have decided that I will go."

"When?"

"I sail just a week from to-day. I wrote yesterday to engage my passage."

"So soon?" Lillian cried, catching her breath, and losing all her brilliant color.

"Yes; if I am to join that excursion to the Pacific coast on the 12th of next month, I must be off."

"The house will seem like a convent when you are gone; you are the life and soul of everything here," said the girl, tears starting to her eyes.

"Thank you; I had no idea that I was of so much importance," he returned, lightly.

"Didn't you?" she asked, sweeping him a coy look from beneath her long, dark lashes. "You have something to learn yet, then. But how long will you be away? Surely not six months, as Uncle Will said this morning."

"Yes, I think so. I do not wish to hurry, and I mean to get a pretty thorough idea of what the United States are like. I think I shall be away until July or August."

"Oh, Rupert, don't! It will be too lonely and wretched for anything without you!" Lillian burst forth, impetuously, and in an agitated voice.

"Why, Lillian!" he exclaimed, astonished, and bestowing a puzzled look upon her downcast, agitated countenance; "will you miss me like that?"

"Did you expect you could go away for so long and not be missed?" she asked, tremulously.

"I confess I had not thought much about it," he replied, gravely; "but I suppose, as we have all been brought up together, and had so much in common, that no one of us could go away without being missed. However, you will have Percy."

"But Percy is soon to go to the Grange, and will be so taken up with his interests there that we shall see but very little of him. Oh, Rupert, I wish there was no such place as America!" Lillian concluded, with quivering lips.

"Bless you, little sister! I never thought that my going away would upset you like this," Rupert said, laying his hand lightly on her shoulder, and really moved to see how she was taking it to heart.

"Little sister!" she repeated, flushing crimson, and drawing her figure to its full height.

She was very handsome at that moment, and Rupert wondered that he had not noticed of late how exceedingly lovely she had grown, while there was a nameless something in her expressive face, and even in her attitude, that thrilled him strangely.

"Does that offend your young ladyship?" he questioned, laughing. "You are not so little after all, and I was unfortunate in my choice of an adjective; but you were such a tiny midget when I came here, eight years ago, that I have always regarded you as very *petite*."

"But I am not—your sister; we are not related at all," she murmured.

He started, and bent a puzzled look upon her. She was standing before him, with half-averted face, her darkly fringed lids almost touching her cheeks, her bosom heaving with the heavy pulsations of her heart.

"True," he returned, in a constrained tone, "and you must pardon me if I have presumed too far; but you must understand, Lillian, that it has become a natural consequence for me to regard you almost in that light, since one cannot live so many years in a family without becoming strongly attached to its members. I had flattered myself, too, that I had won at least a little corner in the hearts of my friends here."

"You have! you have! Oh, Rupert, I did not mean anything like that!" Lillian cried, in a distressed tone, and with visible agitation.

"Then what did you mean? I do not understand you," the young man asked, and leaned forward to look into her downcast face.

Lillian lifted her great dark eyes to his for an instant, and his heart gave a startled bound at what he read in their dusky depths. Then the rich blood rushed in a crimson flood to her very brow, dyeing even her white neck with its rosy hue.

At that moment a door of the conservatory opened and shut, and the girl started guiltily from his side.

"There comes the gardener," she said, with evident confusion, "and I must speak to him."

She darted away, speeding swiftly down the walk, leaving the young man speechless and amazed at the discovery that he had made; for he had read in the girl's beautiful face and speaking glance the confession of her love for him.

"Whew!" he ejaculated, recovering himself after a moment; "I never dreamed of anything like that! What in the world have I been thinking of not to realize before she had grown a young lady, and a very beautiful one, too? I wonder if I could—can it be possible that I have—bah! I never have meant to do any mischief in that way. Perhaps I'll—no, I'll wait until I get back from my trip. It is very awkward. I wish it had not happened just now," he soliloquized, brokenly.

He stood gazing out of the conservatory in an absent way for several minutes, his face very grave, an anxious look in his fine eyes; but, as he heard Lillian and the gardener approaching, he passed around to another path and so out of the hot-house, and thus avoided meeting them; he did not feel that he could encounter the young girl again just then. He wished to get away by himself and think over the revelation he had just received.

The thought of love in connection with Lillian Linton had never entered his mind until now.

She had simply been a genial playmate during the earlier years of his life, sharing many of his own and Percy's sports, and a pleasant companion when, of late, he had returned to Heathdale from college to spend his vacations.

He had scarcely realized—as his own words betrayed—that she had reached woman's estate. He knew she was very pretty, very bright and sparkling; he knew that Heathdale would not seem like home to him without her, and he enjoyed her society as he would that of a dear sister; but as for anything nearer, as a wife, he had never thought of her.

More and more he regretted that little episode in the conservatory. The memory of it embarrassed him, try hard as he would to overcome it, and he found himself avoiding the possibility of a *tête-à-tête* with Lillian again, while he began to grow anxious for the day of his departure, that he might escape the unnatural constraint that seemed to have fallen upon him.

Sir William wondered what had come over him during the next few days, but attributed his unusual gravity to his regret at the approaching separation.

Lady Linton knew from Lillian's manner, that something had gone wrong; but, although she questioned her, she could learn nothing satisfactory, and she became more and more unreconciled over Rupert's projected tour.

If she could only have succeeded in arranging an engagement between him and Lillian before he left, she would have felt quite safe in letting him go; he would have stood committed then, and it would have been a safeguard during his absence.

She did everything in her power to make it pleasant for him during the little time that remained to him at home; she meant that he should at least take away agreeable memories with him, and he assured her again and again that he should never forget her kindness to him, for all that she was doing for him.

"You have been like a mother to me, Lady Linton, ever since I came to Heathdale," he said, gratefully, to her one day when she was arranging something for his comfort during the voyage.

"And you have been like a son to me, my dear boy," she returned, with a fond glance. "I shall always regard you as such. I am sure I do not know what we are going to do without you."

"Six months will soon pass," Rupert said, trying to speak lightly.

"They may to you, who will be traveling constantly, but they will be long to us who wait at home. Poor Lillian! I set her to marking some handkerchiefs for you this morning, but she broke down and cried so over her work that she had to give it up."

"I am afraid I am an unworthy subject for so much regret," Rupert said, with a sigh.

Lillian's regard for him, her pale, sad face, and hollow eyes, were a great burden on his heart.

The day of his departure arrived, and he took an affectionate leave of his friends.

Lady Linton embraced him as fervently as if he had indeed been her son, bade him take care of himself and come safely back to them, for it would break their hearts to lose him entirely. Percy wished him every possible pleasure, and promised to write to him every week. Lillian gave him an icy cold hand at parting; there were tears on her dark lashes, and her lips quivered painfully over her farewell; but she would not allow him to kiss her in the old friendly fashion, as he used to do when he and Percy went back to school at the end of their holidays. She had vowed that their lips should never meet again until he had given her a lover's kiss.

Rupert looked troubled at being thus repulsed. He understood the reason for it, however, and it was with a feeling of relief that he realized he was to have six months in which to make up his mind as to what his duty was toward his guardian's niece.

Sir William accompanied him to London, thence to Liverpool, where he saw him safely on board the stanch Cunarder that was to bear him across the Atlantic, after which he returned to Heathdale, feeling as if half the sunshine had suddenly been blotted from his life. The boy was inexpressibly dear to him, and he would have been bereaved indeed if anything happened to him.

CHAPTER IX.
A STRANGE MEETING.

The voyage was a tempestuous one, but the steamer made her time notwithstanding, and Rupert landed in New York eight days after leaving Liverpool, and was not sorry to be once more upon *terra firma*.

He joined the Raymond party on the twelfth of January, according to his plans, and found himself among a very pleasant company of gentlemen and ladies, young men and maidens, all enthusiastic in view of their trip.

He was particularly attracted by the appearance of one young man, who, like himself, was traveling alone, and after one or two interviews, being mutually pleased with each other, they decided to become traveling companions.

On the third day after starting Rupert's new friend, who, by the way, had introduced himself as Harry Webster, remarked to him:

"I say, Hamilton, have you noticed that dainty little piece of humanity opposite, who is traveling with that old codger, Mr. Knight, they call him?"

"Yes; she is a very attractive young lady," Rupert answered, as his eyes wandered to a trio who occupied seats a little in front of the young men on the opposite side of the car. "I wonder who she is."

"Our list will probably tell us," remarked Mr. Webster, as he drew the card from his pocket. "Yes, I have found it. Mr. Robert G. Knight, Miss E. F. Knight, and Miss Virginia Alexander."

"Ah, then the old gentleman and lady must be brother and sister, and the young lady some friend, perhaps a niece, who is traveling with them," said Rupert.

"The old gentleman appears to be remarkably fond of her though," returned Mr. Webster.

"Yes; but the old lady keeps guard over her as if she feared that some brigand was in ambush, waiting to abduct her pretty charge to regions unknown," Rupert responded with a roguish twinkle in his eye.

"What do you say to making a raid upon the party?" proposed his companion. "Now I am bent upon getting acquainted with that pretty girl, if for nothing more than to show that prim spinster that I can do it. Will you join me, or does such a proposition shock your English ideas of etiquette?"

"I confess I should prefer to have a formal introduction," Rupert returned, flushing slightly, but regarding that graceful figure with a look of unmistakable admiration.

The maiden whom the young men had been discussing was indeed a very lovely girl, about eighteen years of age. She was a trifle above the medium height, having a slender, willowy figure, with a peculiar grace and animation in every movement. Her glossy brown hair was twisted into a shining coil at the back of her head, which was crowned with a pretty hat of gray felt, trimmed with velvet of the same shade and a single scarlet wing. She wore a closely fitting ulster, trimmed with fur, which showed her perfect form to great advantage; a plain linen collar was fastened at her throat with a brooch of dull red gold, and tiny ornaments of the same metal were in her small ears. Her eyes were a dark brown, and quick and restless in their glances; her features were beautifully clear and delicate; the glow of perfect health was on her cheeks; her lips were a vivid red and her complexion very pure.

She was a vivacious little body, laughing and chatting with the elderly gentleman, in whose charge she appeared to be, in a way that betrayed she stood in no fear of him, while his fond glances and the many attentions he bestowed upon her plainly betrayed that he was indeed very fond of her.

Young Webster had been especially attracted toward this party from the hour of starting, and had been on the alert to make their acquaintance, although he had not mentioned the subject before; but the trio had kept pretty well by themselves and appeared quite contented with their own company, so, as yet, there had been no opportunity for him to approach them without making himself conspicuous in so doing.

But in spite of his boast that he would make Miss Alexander's acquaintance, he was destined to be outdone and thrown into the background by his more modest English friend.

When the party was summoned to dinner that day there was the usual rush for the dining-car; human nature will not always be curbed when people are hungry; but Mr. Knight and his companions lingered to avoid the crowd.

Mr. Webster also delayed, and held his friend back in the hope that something might occur to establish an acquaintance with the young lady whom he so much admired.

And something did occur.

In passing from one car to the other, Mr. Knight first assisted his sister across, then turned to his young charge, when a gust of wind whirled her pretty hat from her head, it being held in place only by a pin, and it would have been wafted beyond recovery but for Rupert, who was directly behind her, and who deftly caught it in its flight.

He instantly returned it to its fair owner, saying, with a bow and his frank smile:

"I am very glad that I was quick enough to save it."

"I am glad, too," returned the little lady, with a merry laugh. "Thank you. It would be very awkward to have to go on my way bare-headed."

Rupert glanced at her as she restored the hat to its place with a look which plainly said that he thought it a very pretty head, even in that state.

Mr. Knight politely acknowledged his obligations for the service; but his sister, who was looking over his shoulder, regarded the two young men askance, as if she was not quite sure that the occurrence had not been all a plot, to which old Boreas had craftily lent his aid.

Then they all passed into the dining-room car, where there was one small table unoccupied, with space for four persons, with only one other vacancy at another, midway of the car.

Mr. Knight turned to Rupert, saying, cordially:

"Come and share our table—I see the others are nearly full—and let me introduce you to my sister and ward. What shall I call you, if you please?"

Rupert drew forth a card, and handed it to the gentleman.

"Ah, Mr. Hamilton. My name is Knight. This lady," turning to the spinster, "is my sister, and this gay young woman," with a fond glance into the pretty face beside him, "to whom you have just rendered so signal a service, allow me to introduce as Miss Alexander, Mr. Hamilton."

The young couple acknowledged the introduction, though with heightened color, and then Mr. Knight motioned them to their seats, while Mr. Webster, feeling somewhat chagrined to find that he was being left in the lurch, hastened on to the vacant place farther down, giving his friend a comical glance of recognized defeat as he passed.

Rupert found his new acquaintances very delightful people. Even the spinster, whom he and Webster had laughingly pronounced a "female ogre," proved to be a lady of rare culture and an exceedingly entertaining companion. He was seated beside her, consequently his conversation was mostly with her, although Miss Alexander was his *vis-à-vis*, and he found it almost impossible to keep his eyes away from her dimpled, expressive face.

"How are you enjoying your journey thus far, Mr. Hamilton?" Mr. Knight inquired, during the meal.

"Very much, thank you, although I have no doubt I should enjoy it much better if I were not quite such a stranger to the party."

"We are all strangers for that matter," returned the elder gentleman. "I have noticed that you and your young friend keep much by yourselves; but you must stir about and get acquainted."

"One does not like to intrude upon family parties," Rupert replied, modestly.

"You must not stand upon formality. I have tried to impress that upon my sister here, who is a trifle shy about making new acquaintances; but in such a company as this we all expect to become acquainted with each other, and we shall enjoy our trip much better than to be ceremonious. At all events, I have broken the ice for you; I find it pleasant to have young people about me, and shall be glad to know you better. Eh, Virgie, it has been a little lonely, hasn't it, to have only two old fogies to talk to?" and Mr. Knight turned, with a roguish twinkle in his eyes, to the fair maiden at his side.

The young girl shot a quick glance at Rupert, a charming smile wreathing her red lips.

Then her cheeks began to dimple and her eyes to gleam with mirth.

"I know of one 'old fogy' who is fishing for a compliment," she retorted, with a saucy toss of her bright head, "and who has been speaking two words for himself and one for others. I know what he wants. Mr. Hamilton, do you play whist? Because if you do," she went on, archly, without waiting for him to reply, "and are fond of it, it will be all right; for you will doubtless be invited by my guardian to 'take a hand,' and once committed, look out for yourself; he is an inveterate player, and he has no mercy on his foes."

"Oh, fie! Virgie, what a character to give your best friend; and to a stranger, too," laughed Mr. Knight, good-humoredly; "but I confess I am a dear lover of whist, Mr. Hamilton, and"—with a quizical look at Virgie—"if you know the game, won't you and your friend take a hand, after dinner, with me and my ward? My sister does not play."

"There! I told you so," interposed the gay girl, with a ripple of silvery laughter.

Rupert joined her heartily.

"I thank you for your timely warning, Miss Alexander," he said, "but I do understand the game and like it, too; but before I commit myself, won't you tell me, please, is your friend a very formidable antagonist?"

"Dreadful! he plays as if his life and honor depended upon his winning every game," she answered, the dimples playing at hide and seek about her lovely mouth, while Rupert thought her the most delightful little body he had ever met.

"Then perhaps you may know some of the weak points of the enemy, and will join me in besieging his fort after dinner," he said, with an appealing glance.

"Thank you; I will, with pleasure, Mr. Hamilton," was the gay response; "it is not often that I play against him; but if I could see him beaten a few times, just to take some of what our Irish neighbors call 'the consate' out of him, I think I should rather enjoy it."

"Oh! the depravity of human nature!" cried Mr. Knight, in mock distress, though his eyes rested very tenderly upon the bright face beside him; "after sharing all my honors in the past, to forswear your allegiance like this! it is rank treason."

"Do not be disheartened, my dear guardian," laughed Virgie, "for perhaps you have it in your power to punish me severely for my presumption in taking up arms against you; however, Mr. Hamilton, we will do our best to come off victorious."

When they returned to the palace car, Rupert introduced his friend, and then the quartet gave themselves up to the enjoyment of their cards, Miss Knight occupying a seat in another section, and burying herself in a book.

They played for two or three hours, and to Miss Virgie's great glee, she and her partner beat the others three games out of five.

Mr. Knight accepted his defeat very good-naturedly, but declared that he would be even with them some other time, and then he fell into conversation with his new acquaintances upon the topics of the day, while Virgie sat by and listened, and studied the two young men in whose society she had been so unexpectedly thrown.

Of course we all recognize in Mr. Knight the great publisher, who had been so kind to Mrs. Alexander, in San Francisco, during her many trials there.

The beautiful girl who is traveling with him is her daughter, Virgie, who, when we last saw her at Niagara, was but ten years of age. She is now eighteen, and blossoming into lovely womanhood, and as charming and winsome a maiden as one could find, go the world over.

Her home for a number of years had been in New York city, her mother, as we know, having changed her residence at the time that Mr. Knight decided to come East to establish himself in business.

Mrs. Alexander had used her pen during all this time, giving her friend one or two little gems of art every year, for it was a pleasant pastime for her to employ herself in this way, but her chief thought had been given to the education of her daughter, who proved to be bright and intelligent beyond the average nineteenth century girl. She had graduated from one of the select schools of the city during the summer just passed, and her mother had begun to contemplate taking her abroad when spring should come again, with the intention of demanding her right at Heathdale.

Still, as the time gradually drew nearer, she had shrunk more and more from the task before her, until the constant dread of it had begun to affect her health, and she had been far from well during the last few months.

Mr. Knight and his sister had never visited San Francisco since leaving that city, although they had often talked of doing so. But this winter, when they learned of the Raymond excursion to that and other points on the Pacific coast, they proposed to join it, and invited Mrs. Alexander and her daughter to accompany them.

She did not feel equal to either the weariness or the excitement of the journey; but she thought that it would be a good opportunity for Virgie to visit the far West, and she gladly confided her to the care of her friends for the two months that the trip would occupy, and thus we find her in company with Mr. and Mrs. Knight, bound for the State where her mother had been born, and as fate had strangely ordered it, with the very party which Sir William Heath's ward, Rupert Hamilton, had joined.

CHAPTER X.
MR. AND MISS KNIGHT VERSUS CUPID.

The ice once broken between Mr. Knight's party and the two young men, the acquaintance progressed rapidly, and it soon became evident that Rupert and Virgie found each other especially congenial.

The young Englishman managed to constitute himself the beautiful girl's escort upon almost every occasion when they were sight-seeing, until Mr. Webster began to realize that he was *de trop*, or as he humorously expressed it, but the "fifth wheel to the coach," and he was forced to look about him for other society to soothe his wounded pride.

He soon found it in the companionship of two sisters, who were traveling with an aunt, and the dark eyes and sparkling beauty of the elder ere long bade fair to make as much a captive of him as Virgie had already made of Rupert Hamilton.

She was the loveliest girl that he had ever seen. Lillian Linton, and the startling discovery which Rupert had made regarding her feelings toward himself just before leaving Heathdale, were forgotten, and he surrendered himself to the charm of her society, never questioning to what it might lead, or what his feelings might be when the trip was ended, and they should go their different ways.

But others began to consider these things if the youthful couple did not.

Older and more experienced eyes could see that he was fast learning to love the charming girl, and that she was also yielding her young heart, with its first strong passion, to the handsome Englishman.

Mr. and Miss Knight could not fail to perceive the danger that lurked in the pleasant companionship, and, while they liked the frank, manly fellow uncommonly well, they were troubled at the thought of anything serious growing out of it, while Virgie was in their care.

"Robert, I am afraid there is mischief brewing, and I feel very uneasy about it," Miss Knight remarked to her brother one day, as Rupert and Virgie stole away together to a corner of the parlor in the hotel where they were stopping to look over a collection of views, which the young man had recently purchased.

Mr. Knight shot a keen, anxious look at them.

"I've been a little fearful of it myself, Stella," he replied, gravely; "but I do not know as we can prevent it."

"We must prevent it," returned his sister, firmly. "We must do our duty, Robert; it would not be right to allow that dear child to become entangled in a love affair while she is away from her mother. I should never forgive myself, and she would never forgive us, if any harm should befall her while she is in our care."

"I cannot think there is anything wrong about the young chap," returned Mr. Knight, his eyes resting thoughtfully on the handsome face looking so smilingly into Virgie's; "he seems like a fine, manly fellow and has no bad habits; he does not even smoke, which is a rare virtue among young men nowadays."

"But we know nothing about him or his family," persisted the lady; "we do not even know from what portion of England he came; at least I do not."

"Neither do I," said her brother; "I have never questioned him and he seems very modest about talking of himself; but if Virgie were my daughter—and you know that I love her almost as well as if she were—I do not think I should feel very much alarmed to have her fall in love with as noble a specimen of manhood as young Hamilton appears to be."

"I like him, too, Robert," said Miss Knight; "he is every inch a gentleman, and doubtless belongs to a good family or he would not have been so carefully reared. Still I am troubled; I want Virgie to go home as free as she came, and—I feel as if young Hamilton ought to be put upon his honor—at least until we can give her back to her mother, when, of course, our responsibility will cease. I can read the signs of the times pretty well, if I have grown to be an old woman, and, if we do not look out, they will be acknowledged lovers before another fortnight goes by."

Mr. Knight looked thoughtful.

"Well," he responded after a moment of silence, "we shall not be together much longer. Hamilton leaves this party as soon as we have done California to go to Mexico with another company, so——"

"Yes, I know that," interrupted his sister, "and that is just what is going to precipitate matters if we are not on our guard. When the time comes for them to separate you do not suppose he will leave her without begging for some word of hope?"

"Stella, you reason remarkably well," said Mr. Knight, laughing, "and I think it will be best to put a flea in the boy's ear. I suppose it will be better for me to get the name of being a meddlesome old fogy rather than run any risk of future unhappiness for our dear girl."

Miss Knight appeared to be satisfied with this decision of her brother, and dropped the subject.

The party was at San Jose when this conversation occurred. They were to remain several days in the beautiful city, making it their headquarters also while visiting points of interest in its vicinity, and Mr. Knight resolved to make a bold stroke at once at the disagreeable task that his sister had imposed on him, and have the matter off his mind.

As they were leaving the table of the Anjerais House after dinner that evening he slipped his arm within Rupert's in a confidential way and said, with a genial smile:

"Mr. Hamilton, I am going out for a little quiet stroll about the city; will you come with me?"

Rupert had been meditating a cozy *tête-à-tête* with Virgie on the veranda, while the band discoursed sweet music on the stand near by, but he was too well bred and unselfish to refuse an old gentleman's request, and unhesitatingly responded:

"Thank you, sir, I shall be happy to accompany you."

When they were in the street Mr. Knight turned his steps toward the park near by, and, after walking up and down its beautiful avenues for a while, he seated himself upon a rustic bench and motioned his companion to sit beside him.

Then he turned frankly to him, and, speaking with great kindness, said:

"My young friend, it has always been my practice, when I had any disagreeable duty to perform, to adopt the most straightforward course, and, as I have something on my heart which I wish to say to you, I trust that you will pardon me if I speak out freely."

Rupert Hamilton's heart gave one tremendous bound at these words, and he cast a startled look into the friendly face beside him, knowing intuitively what was coming.

"If I am in any way connected with this disagreeable duty, sir, I hope you will speak frankly," he managed to stammer.

"Thank you. I felt sure that you would receive what I have to say in a friendly spirit," Mr. Knight continued, pitying the embarrassed lover sincerely. "I am an old man, my boy, but I have been young and do not forget the temptations and pleasures belonging to youth; neither can I find it in my heart to blame two charming people for recognizing a congenial spirit, and turning to each other for companionship; but——"

Rupert Hamilton turned now, and looked squarely into his aged friend's countenance.

"In other words, sir, you wish to speak with me regarding my admiration for Miss Alexander, which, of course, I know you have not failed to remark," he said, in a manly, outspoken fashion, that pleased Mr. Knight well, though a deep red flush mantled his cheek.

"You are right, that is just what I wish to confer with you about," the elder gentleman returned, adding, "You will no doubt appreciate the responsibility of my position, when I tell you that Miss Alexander is the only child of a very dear friend, and the young lady was intrusted to my own and my sister's care, during the journey, because her mother was not herself able to accompany her. We therefore feel that it would be very unwise and dishonorable on our part, to allow her to receive, from any one, attentions which might tend to hamper her future in any way. For this reason, I wish to speak a word of caution to you. Virgie is very young, and I do not believe she has given a thought to what might result from this pleasant intercourse, and I should deeply regret it if she should become involved in any affair of the heart while away from her mother."

"You are right, sir;" Rupert answered, gravely, after a moment of thought, "and I thank you for your timely admonition, else, in a moment of impulse, I might have been led to betray more of my regard for Miss Alexander than would be wise or right, under the circumstances. I will deal as frankly with you, as you have dealt with me, and confess that I admire her more than any young lady I have ever met. She is very lovely, and"—the flush on his handsome face deepening—"were you her father instead of her temporary guardian, I should boldly ask your permission to address her with the hope of some day winning her affection."

Mr. Knight smiled upon the eager lover.

"I imagine that I have spoken none too soon," he said. "I am afraid that sly little god, Cupid, has already wrought more mischief than I will be able to remedy. But I admire your candor, Mr. Hamilton, and if you desire a more intimate acquaintance with my pretty little ward, by and by, I will give you her address and you can seek her in her own home, where there will be no ogre to rear obstacles in your path."

"Do not call yourself hard names, Mr. Knight," Rupert said, regarding him with a look of profound respect. "I am sure you have done only what you believe to be right."

"Thank you; you may be assured that it was not an agreeable duty," returned the publisher, with a shrug of his shoulders, adding, with a roguish twinkle in his eyes, "and if Virgie were my daughter I think you would not have found me a very obdurate parent. Truly, young man, I like you exceedingly well, and when we go back to New York, I will do all in my power to favor your suit, if you are then of the same mind as now."

"You are very kind, sir," Rupert said, gratefully, "and now, as I may not have another opportunity to make the request, if you will give me Miss Alexander's address, I shall consider it a favor."

Mr. Knight drew forth a card and wrote it for him, wondering why he should speak as he had done about not having another opportunity to get it.

A little later they returned to the hotel, where Rupert at once sought the manager of the excursion, and did not join the company again for an hour or more.

Then it seemed as if a change had come over him. He was quiet and preoccupied, almost spiritless. Virgie noticed it, and wondered what could have occurred to make him so. He did not devote himself as exclusively as usual to her, although he was never far away from her.

When the party broke up for the night, after an unusually merry evening, he went to her with a sinking heart.

She looked up at him with shy eyes and a dimpling smile, that almost made him break a resolve that he had made since he last saw her.

"You have not been like yourself this evening, Mr. Hamilton," she said. "Have you had bad news, or are you not quite well?"

"Neither, Miss Alexander," he replied, looking down upon her bright face with eyes that kindled and glowed in spite of the restraint that he was imposing on himself. "I am simply experiencing a good deal of regret that I must leave some of my pleasant companions; I am going to join a party for Mexico immediately."

"Are you?" Virgie asked, with a start, and looking greatly surprised, while she lost some of her lovely color.

She thought it very singular that he had not before mentioned the fact of his intention to leave at this point. She knew that later on he was intending to go farther South.

"Yes," he said, his heart beating heavily, as he read the regret in her eyes. "Some gentlemen have arranged for an ocean trip, intending to touch at the Santa Barbara Islands and land at San Diego, whence they will proceed into Mexico. I am going with them."

All the light had died out of Virgie's face during this explanation. It seemed as if there was nothing left for her to enjoy during the remainder of the tour.

She had never realized before how dependent for enjoyment she had been upon his society, and now he was going another way. Perhaps they would never meet again; he would doubtless go directly back to England after his return from Mexico, and that would end this delightful episode of her life.

Her heart cried out against the separation, and, like a flash, it came to her how much this frank, noble young Englishman had become to her.

She did not know what to say to him; she stood there silent, wretched, and pale as the snowy lace that lay in folds upon her white neck.

"You—have changed your plans quite suddenly, have you not?" she at last managed to stammer.

"It is rather an unexpected move," he tried to say, in a natural tone; "but I may never have another opportunity to take a voyage upon the Pacific Ocean, and it seems best that I should go."

It would have taken but very little more to have broken the fair girl down entirely. In all her life she had scarcely known a trial, hardly a wish ungratified, and this had come upon her like a thunderbolt from the sky.

She knew that she ought to make no sign before him, and yet she could not repress all feeling.

Her lips quivered slightly and there was a wistful expression in her eyes as she lifted them to him and said:

"I am sorry that you are going, Mr. Hamilton. We shall miss you sadly."

"Shall you?" he cried, eagerly, his face growing luminous. "Thank you," he added, checking himself again. "I am sorry, too, to leave you; but, Miss Alexander, I shall be in New York early in the spring. May I hope to renew our acquaintance there? May I come to see you in your own home?"

A rosy glow leaped into the young girl's face at this request. A heavy load dropped from her heart, a sweet, new hope began to bud within her soul.

"Yes, indeed; do come, Mr. Hamilton. I know that mamma will be glad to meet you," she said, cordially.

"Thank you; but will you also be glad to see me, Vir—Miss Alexander?" the young man asked, in a low, eager tone, and there was an expression in his eyes of which he was wholly unconscious, but which told his fair companion much that he had fully intended should remain hidden deep within his own heart until he could stand before Mrs. Alexander, tell her how tenderly he had learned to love her daughter, and ask her sanction to his suit.

"Yes, I shall be glad," Virgie breathed, softly, her white lids hiding the happy light in her eyes, though there was a tell-tale glow upon her cheek.

Some one was approaching them and he knew he must leave her, though she had never seemed so lovely to him as in that shy, sweet mood.

"I leave early to-morrow morning, therefore I must say good-night and good-by now," he said, trying to smile as he extended his hand to her, though his voice was a trifle unsteady.

She laid hers within it and looked up archly, as she replied:

"I shall not say good-by to you, Mr. Hamilton. I do not like the words. I will bid you good speed, wishing you a pleasant voyage and a safe return."

His fingers closed over the small hand with a fond, lingering clasp, then with one last look into her dear face, he turned away, to make his adieus elsewhere, knowing that he should not see her again for months, but feeling as if his soul had quaffed some strangely inspiring elixir during that last moment or two in her sweet presence.

CHAPTER XI.
A BITTER DISAPPOINTMENT.

It seemed very dull to Virgie for a while after the departure of Rupert, who had been a very lively and agreeable traveler; indeed, the whole company missed him; but Mr. Knight and his sister exerted themselves to fill the young man's place as far as possible, and, with the memory of that last interview, and the hope of meeting him again in New York in the spring, Virgie resolved not to pine, and gave herself up to the hearty enjoyment of her sight-seeing and other pleasures of the journey.

The trip proved to be a most enjoyable one in every way, and when Virgie returned to her mother, in March, looking rosy and happy, and full of life and enthusiasm over what she had recently seen, Mrs. Alexander felt well repaid for the loneliness she had experienced during this, their first separation.

Mr. Knight told her confidentially of Rupert Hamilton and his evident admiration for her charming daughter, and warned her that she might look for the young man's return about the first or middle of May.

Mrs. Alexander was at first inclined to laugh over the romantic episode, until her friend mentioned that Rupert was an Englishman, whereupon she grew very grave and sad.

"I hope they will never meet again," she said, sternly. "I do not want my child to marry an Englishman; it is enough that her mother's heart was broken by one of that nationality."

"Surely, my friend, you do not imagine that all Englishmen are knaves simply because one has proved himself such?" said Mr. Knight.

"I suppose I have no right to judge them so, yet I have a prejudice against them that I cannot overcome," responded Mrs. Alexander, with a sigh. "I hope my darling, if she ever marries, will become the wife of a stanch American."

"The young man is a noble specimen of his countrymen, I can assure you," Mr. Knight answered, anxious to do Rupert justice. "I confess I should be rather proud of him for a son-in-law."

Mrs. Alexander sighed heavily, and did not reply; but she secretly resolved that if it was in her power to prevent it, Virgie and her English admirer should never meet again.

April passed and May came, and Virgie began to grow expectant. She was blooming into brighter beauty with every day, and seemed to become more womanly, so that her mother felt, with something of sadness, that she no longer had her little girl, but a lovely and winsome maiden, who would doubtless soon be won from her sheltering care to grace the home of another.

She had been a beautiful child, but she was far lovelier now, possessing her mother's refined and delicate features and graceful figure, while her eyes were so like her father's that her mother often suffered keenest pain as she looked into them, and seemed to be gazing again through them into the heart of the man whom she had loved so fondly in her youth.

Of late she had pined anew for the affection which had guarded her so tenderly in those early years.

Perhaps it was because her health had not been as firm as usual during the last few months. She felt weary and depressed. She longed for some one to lean upon—some one strong and true to shield her from the cares and worry of life.

Every day, during the first two weeks of May, Virgie watched for the coming of Rupert Hamilton.

She knew that he expected to return to New York about this time, and she felt sure that he would seek her at once, while she believed that his coming would mean a great deal to her. There was an eager, expectant look on her young face, a deeper flush in her cheeks, a bright and hopeful light in her eyes.

Mrs. Alexander read the signs of the time well, and realized that the hour for her to act had come.

The warm weather was very enervating to her. She drooped visibly, and calling her physician she asked his advice regarding some change of residence.

He advised her to leave the city immediately; to go to some quiet country place where she could have pure air, fresh, rich milk, and a nourishing diet.

Consequently she decided to seek a lovely place on the Hudson, where she had spent a summer several years previous, and where she could be as quiet as she chose, and rest the livelong day if she wished.

Miss Knight decided to accompany her, for her brother feared that the woman whom he still regarded with far more than mere friendly feelings, was more frail than she acknowledged herself to be, and he thought she ought to have some one more experienced than Virgie with her in the event of any more serious illness.

Mr. Knight himself was contemplating a trip through the New England States, but promised to join them and spend the remainder of the summer with them upon his return.

Poor Virgie was made very unhappy upon learning of these plans, for it destroyed her hope of meeting Rupert Hamilton, who, she believed, was even now upon his way back to New York.

She did not, however, pose a single objection to her mother's plans, for the doctor had said her health demanded an immediate change, and she was not selfish enough to wish to delay a single hour, even though her going might blight the fondest hopes of her life.

But she could not deceive the keen eyes of love, and Mrs. Alexander was quick to note her paling cheek, the thoughtful, wistful look upon her hitherto bright face, and she realized with a bitter pang that already her darling's heart had responded to a stronger affection than hers.

But it made her all the more eager to hasten her departure, and on the fifteenth of May they left New York for their summer home upon the Hudson.

Thus it will be seen that Rupert, who arrived in New York only a few days later, missed them, and was cut off entirely from all communication with Virgie.

He sought Mr. Knight upon the very day of his arrival, but was greatly disappointed to learn that he had left the city. He then repaired to the address which he had given him, hoping to find Virgie, but the house was closed; and though he inquired at one or two places, no one could tell whither Mrs. Alexander and her daughter had gone.

Life seemed to grow suddenly dark to him then, for he had been looking forward to this hour with a great deal of hope. It had been no light struggle for him to break away from the party at San Jose as he had done, and only a sense of honor and his own weakness had enabled him to do so.

He knew that he loved Virgie Alexander with the one strong passion of his life, and that if he had continued the journey with her he must have told her so. Mr. Knight's conversation with him, however, had convinced him that this would be wrong, and so the only thing that remained for him was to get out of the way of temptation. But during all his journey he had looked forward to the day when, in her mother's presence, he could honorably proclaim his affection, which only strengthened with every passing day, and win her for his wife.

He remained in New York for two or three weeks, hoping to learn something of either Mr. Knight or the Alexanders; but he failed to do so, and then turned his face in another direction, resolving to prolong his stay in America until fall, with the hope of finding Virgie, when he should again return to New York before sailing for England.

He spent the summer in visiting the New England States, the great lakes, and some portions of Canada. He saw much to interest him, but was conscious all the time of one intense longing, one unsatisfied desire, and it was with a feeling of relief that, at the beginning of October, he found himself once more in New York.

Sir William was very impatient for his return, and had written charging him to take passage as early as possible for home, for there was to be a great celebration at Heathdale on the twentieth of the month to commemorate the fiftieth anniversary of the founding of an orphans' home.

Consequently Rupert's first duty was to engage his stateroom for his return voyage, the steamer advertising to sail on the eighth.

Then he again instituted inquiries for his friends, but none of them had yet returned, neither was he able to discover their summer resort, and thus the eighth of October came, and, with a sadder heart than he ever possessed, Rupert went on board the Cephalonia to return to his native land.

How many times Sir William Heath had turned his face homeward with just the same despair at his heart; the same moody brow, and pained, anxious face; the same intense longing for the woman whom he loved better than life itself!

But the end was not yet.

CHAPTER XII.
AN UNEXPECTED MEETING.

Rupert stood at the stern of the vessel as the last bell rang, and she slowly swung out from her moorings and began to steam down the harbor.

His arms were tightly folded across his chest, which seemed laden with a hundred-pound weight; his face was pale and stern, his eyes moody and fixed upon the receding domes and spires of the great city that he had just left.

There was a conflict of emotions in his soul, and rebellion was the fiercest of them all—rebellion against his bitter disappointment and the unrequited love that filled his heart.

He never moved from his post for an hour; he had no interest in anything that was transpiring about him; he knew, or thought he knew, no one on board, and he had no desire for society just then, even if he had; he cared little or nothing about the location of his stateroom, or to learn who were to be his companions during the next eight days.

The day was perfect. It had been oppressively warm in the city, but there was a delightful breeze upon the ocean and the air was delicious. There was not a cloud to be seen, and the sun shone around that floating world in matchless splendor, tipping every wave and ripple made by the motion of the vessel with gleams of silver, while beyond the waters were darkly and beautifully blue.

But the young man was not conscious of any of this beauty, and he might have stood there still another hour, absorbed in his own sorrowful reflections, but for a little circumstance that startled and shocked him into new life.

A voice near him was saying:

"Mamma, do you think you would like to sit here? this life-boat makes a nice shelter. I will arrange your chair and wraps, and I am sure you will be comfortable."

"It looks inviting," was the pleasant rejoinder; "I will at least try it until I begin to experience those qualms which all voyagers so much dread."

A merry little laugh rang out at this—a laugh that made Rupert Hamilton's blood tingle and glow, and his heart beat with quickened throbs; then the first voice responded:

"We are not going to have any qualms, mamma. I am determined to be a good sailor, and I will not hear a word about your being sick. Why, what should I do for company without you, and not a friend to speak to on this great ship?"

Rupert turned now to look at the speaker, his face luminous with surprise and delight; the moody look all gone from his brow, his fine lips wreathed with smiles.

At this movement the young girl glanced up and their eyes met.

"Miss Alexander!" cried the young man, going forward with outstretched hand.

"Mr. Hamilton!" Virgie stammered, her lovely face suffused with blushes.

Their hands met in an eager clasp, and Mrs. Alexander, viewing this unexpected reunion of the youth and maiden from her position a little in the background, and noting how much their looks and actions expressed, knew that she had run directly into the danger she had been trying to escape all summer.

But it was too late to mend matters now; fate had ordered it so to be, and she could only submit to the inevitable with as good a grace as possible.

"Mamma," Virgie said, as soon as she could collect herself, "this is Mr. Hamilton, whom we met during the trip to California; Mr. Hamilton, let me introduce you to my mother, Mrs. Alexander."

The lady and gentleman exchanged greetings, and then Rupert insisted upon making himself useful to Mrs. Alexander, who was still something of an invalid, although much better than when we last saw her in May.

He unfolded her chair, saw her comfortably seated, and then arranged her wraps and rugs so deftly, and was so kindly attentive to her needs, so gentlemanly and entertaining in conversation, that she was at once disarmed of half her fears and prejudices.

"He is really a very charming young man," she admitted to herself, as she lay back among her robes and watched his expressive face while he talked with Virgie. "I do not wonder that she became interested in him, and, perhaps, after all, if she is to live in England, it might be as well for her to make an English alliance; I hope his family is a good one."

That a great deal of mischief, if it could be regarded as such, had been done during those few weeks of travel in the West was plainly apparent.

Rupert showed his happiness over this unexpected meeting in every look and gesture. One could hardly believe him to be the same person, who, half an hour previous, had stood like some stern statue looking back in despair upon the city he was leaving behind; while as for Virgie, her mother scarcely knew her for the drooping, pale-faced damsel that she had been all summer, although she had not been guilty of a single murmur.

Mrs. Alexander's health had improved somewhat, but she was far from strong even yet, and her physician had urgently advised an ocean voyage.

She had demurred at first, but when he said, "Your daughter, too, needs the change; I do not like her looks at all," her mother-love prevailed, and she nerved herself for her long contemplated voyage to England, feeling that perhaps the proper time had come for her to act in the matter of Virgie's inheritance, and thus it chanced—if chance it was—that they were booked for the same steamer in which Rupert had sailed.

But, alas! for Virgie's boast that she was "determined to be a good sailor," for she had not been on deck many hours before she was prostrated by that much dreaded enemy of all voyagers, sea-sickness, and thus all the pleasant *tête-à-têtes* and promenades which Rupert had begun to plan immediately upon discovering that she was on board the steamer, came to naught.

The poor girl was hardly able to lift her head from her pillow during the whole voyage, and when they arrived at Liverpool she was so reduced that she had to be carried off the vessel.

She began to rally at once, however, after landing, and continued to improve during the journey to London.

Mrs. Alexander had borne it all wonderfully well, suffering but very little from "qualms," which she had so much dreaded, and Rupert having constituted himself her constant attendant, they had become the best of friends during the eight days that they had spent together.

When they arrived in London, Rupert assisted them in finding pleasant lodgings in an excellent locality, and then began to think of his own friends at Heathdale.

"I shall be in London again soon, and may I beg the privilege of coming to see you occasionally?" he asked, as he was taking leave of the two ladies.

"Yes, indeed, we shall be very glad to see you, Mr. Hamilton," Mrs. Alexander rejoined, cordially, while Virgie blushed with pleasure at the request, and a shy smile dimpled the corners of her pretty mouth. "But," she added, "you have not yet told us whither you are going—in what portion of England is your home."

"I have no home really, as yet, Mrs. Alexander, but I have friends in Hampshire County, and I am going to them for a while," Rupert replied.

As was his custom, he seldom talked about himself, and this was the first intimation that Mrs. Alexander had received of his having friends in Hampshire, where Sir William lived.

She grew a trifle pale as he mentioned the fact, and longed to ask him if he knew the baronet; but she checked herself, and they separated without a suspicion on her part of his being in any way connected with the man whom she had come to England to seek.

Mr. Knight had given her letters of introduction to some friends of his residing in Grosvenor square, and, upon seeking them, she found them to be most delightful people.

Sir Humphrey Huntington and his family occupied a high social position in London, and thus had it in their power to make it very pleasant for any one in whom they were interested.

They tried to persuade Mrs. Alexander to come to them as their guest, instead of remaining in lodgings; but she preferred, for various reasons, to be independent, although she compromised the matter somewhat by frequently allowing Virgie to visit Sir Humphrey's two daughters, who were about her own age.

And now there began a charmed life for Virgie Alexander, as, for the present, we must continue to call her, since her mother did not wish her to be introduced by the name of Heath until she could be assured that she would succeed in having her acknowledged as the heiress of Heathdale.

As soon as she was sufficiently rested, Mrs. Alexander intended to consult with some good lawyer and give her interests into his care; but, meanwhile, she was willing that her darling should enjoy to the utmost the pleasures at hand.

Grace and Helen Huntington were bright and attractive girls, but neither of them possessed a tithe of the beauty which the gods has conferred upon their young guest. They were generous and kind enough, too, not to envy her for it, but rather made a pet of her, and were proud to entertain the fair American, who soon became an acknowledged belle.

The Huntingtons were in the habit of giving fortnightly receptions to some of the *bon ton*, of London, and it was at one of these gatherings that Virgie made her *début* in society.

She had never been much in company, having left school only the previous year, but now she entered into the enjoyment of everything with all the enthusiasm of her girlish nature.

She was very lovely on the evening of her first appearance at a reception at Lady Huntington's.

She came into the great drawing-room leaning on the arm of Helen Huntington, a sparkling brunette, clad in garnet silk.

Virgie's mother had taken great pains with her toilet, and it was absolutely perfect. It was of finest albatross cloth, combined with white satin, fitting her slender form like a glove, and draped in the most artistic manner, while the scarlet flowers, gleaming here and there among the graceful folds, made a very pleasing effect.

Her nut-brown hair was loosely coiled and fastened with a small silver comb, while a few light rings lay in careless array upon her pure forehead. Her dark eyes were gleaming with excitement and anticipation; her cheeks were slightly flushed, and her red lips wreathed with happy smiles.

"Who is that beautiful girl in white, with scarlet verbenas?" asked a distinguished-looking woman, who was conversing with Lady Huntington, as Virgie entered the room.

"She is a young American for whom a friend of my husband bespoke our hospitality and attention."

"Ah!" replied the other, looking interested, and raising her glass for a better view of the stranger. "I might have known. We have few beauties of that delicate type in this country. What is her name?"

But the woman started even as she asked the question, while her glance searched Virgie's face with an eager, wondering look. Something in its delicate outlines and striking beauty seemed to arouse long dormant memories.

"Miss Alexander," said Lady Huntington; "she and her mother arrived from New York only ten days ago. Would you like an introduction? She is very charming, and wonderfully well informed for a girl of her age."

"Um!—yes, presently; but——Sadie, do tell me who she looks like!" and Mrs. Farnum, for it was she, turned to a queenly woman near by, to draw her attention to the fair stranger.

Sadie Farnum, or Lady Royalston, as she was now known, had long since resigned all hope of becoming the mistress of Heathdale, and, having married a wealthy lord twice her age, had given herself up to fashion and society.

"Of whom are you speaking, mamma?"

"Of that girl who is standing beside Helen Huntington. Of whom does she remind you?"

"I am sure I cannot tell," Lady Royalston answered, searching the bright face to which her attention had been called. "It certainly has a familiar look, and yet one that I cannot place. She is very pretty."

Mrs. Farnum did not reply, but continued to follow every movement of that graceful form, every expression of the sweet countenance, while she searched the chambers of her memory for its counterpart and the circumstances under which she had seen it.

Presently the two girls approached Lady Huntington, when she passed her arm around Virgie's slight waist, saying:

"My dear, I wish to introduce you to an old friend who has been inquiring about you. Mrs. Farnum, allow me to present our young guest, Miss Virgie Alexander."

CHAPTER XIII.
RUPERT'S REQUEST.

"Virgie Alexander!" repeated Mrs. Farnum to herself, as she acknowledged the presentation, and it almost seemed as if some one had struck a blow upon her heart as she recalled that long-forgotten name and looked into that delicate, clear-cut face, while a vision from out of the past suddenly rose to confront her.

She saw the tall, slight figure of a beautiful woman very like this young girl, standing straight and proud before her, as, with a face of agony and a voice full of despair, she asserted her own purity and her child's legitimacy, and hurled back scorn for scorn upon the arrogant women who repudiated her claim and tried to crush her with a vile conspiracy.

Again she seemed to hear those ringing, prophetic words, "My child is also the lawful child of Sir William Heath; she is the heiress of Heathdale, and she shall yet occupy the position that rightfully belongs to her. Let your 'peer of the realm and his honored family' take warning; the time will come when a righteous judgment will overtake them."

She shivered slightly as she recalled all this and Virgie wondered what should make the fine-looking woman grow so suddenly pale, and why she should regard her with such a fixed and startled gaze.

But she gave the circumstance only a passing thought, and then turned to speak to Lady Royalston, to whom Lady Huntington also presented her, only to find herself again the object of a curious and astonished stare.

Sadie Farnum turned to her mother as the maiden passed on, and the eyes of the two women, as they met, expressed a great deal.

"Her name is Virgie, and she looks like that woman," whispered Mrs. Farnum, in an agitated voice.

"She certainly does; but Lady Huntington introduced her as Miss Alexander."

"Don't you understand? That was the name of her father—that man who defaulted from the —— bank, in San Francisco."

"True! I had forgotten. But—it cannot be possible that this girl was that baby?"

"Why not? She is just about the age that child would be. You know, it is eighteen years since we were in America."

"So it is. How time does fly!" Lady Royalston remarked, with a sigh of regret for the lost hopes of her youth.

"And, you know, that girl threatened to come to England some time to claim her position."

Mrs. Farnum had confided all the plot against Virgie to her daughter after their return to England, and upon learning that a divorce between Sir William Heath and his wife had been secured, she had gathered fresh hope that Sadie would yet become Lady Heath.

"I know you said she did; but so many years have elapsed without anything happening, I supposed she had given up that idea, particularly as she obtained a divorce."

"She was a high-spirited thing," replied Mrs. Farnum, with a troubled look, "and I believe she procured a legal separation simply to show him that she would not hold him bound if he wished to be free; but I imagine that she has never relinquished the determination to prove her child the heiress of Heathdale. I am afraid Lady Linton's plans will come to grief after all, and if they do, we may become involved in the unpleasant business."

Lady Royalston looked disturbed for a moment, then she replied:

"Pshaw! I would not worry over a fancied resemblance."

"It is not fancied," returned her mother, "it is very striking. You have seen it as well as I."

"Where is the girl's mother?"

"I do not know. Lady Huntington simply said that they arrived from New York ten days ago, bringing a letter to Sir Humphrey from a friend who requested his hospitality for them."

"If that is the case, they must have been moving in good society," remarked Lady Royalston, reflectively.

"Yes; and they must have means. Did you notice the girl's toilet? It was simply exquisite."

"Yes; the finest of everything, and in the best of taste. I cannot understand it, for you told me that Sir William brought all his wife's fortune back to England with him."

"She told me so herself! but she must have found another somewhere, or they could not come here in this style."

"Perhaps she has married again," suggested Lady Royalston.

"No, indeed. Don't you understand? She still retains her maiden name, with simply the 'Mrs.' added. I must find out more about them. I will pump Lady

Huntington again before we leave," Mrs. Farnum concluded, rather inelegantly.

She was as good as her word, but all that she could learn was that Mrs. Alexander had come abroad for her health—that she and her daughter were traveling alone. Lady Huntington believed she was a widow, but judged she must have lost her husband many years ago, since she never mentioned him, and wore no weeds. She said she was not able to go much into society, being still something of an invalid, although much better than before her voyage.

This was not very satisfactory to Mrs. Farnum, and she felt very uneasy.

"I must see the woman for myself," she told her daughter. "I should know her at once, and I shall not rest until I do. I sincerely wish we had never meddled with that wretched business."

"I wish so, too," sighed Lady Royalston, but it was more for her mother's sake than her own, for, as we know, her sympathies had been with the poor young wife when they were together in New York.

But Virgie, all unconscious of the anxiety which her presence had created, was enjoying herself exceedingly.

She attracted a great deal of attention, and was soon surrounded by a group of admirers who vied with each other in doing homage to the lovely young American, while the Misses Huntington appeared to enjoy her conquests as if they were themselves the recipients of similar honors.

But, in the midst of her triumphs, Virgie chanced to glance toward the entrance to the drawing-room and saw standing there a figure that sent all the blood tingling to her finger-tips; and, as she met the eyes that were fixed so admiringly upon her, her own sent back a responsive glance which made Rupert Hamilton forget that there was anyone else in the room and start forward to greet her, regardless of the charmed circle about her which he must pass.

"Miss Alexander!" he said, in a low, earnest tone, "I did not anticipate this pleasure when I came hither to-night."

"And you are a surprise to me," Virgie answered, blushing slightly. "I did not know that you were in town. Have you been well since we parted?"

"Very; and I do not need to ask if you fully recovered from the effects of your voyage," he returned, with a glance that made her pulses leap.

"I am, indeed, very well," she said, "and mamma is also very much improved, although she does not feel quite equal to society yet. Did you find your friends well?"

"Yes, thank you," Rupert answered, but his face fell at the question, for it brought Lillian so forcibly to his mind. She had betrayed so much joy upon his return that he had been painfully embarrassed and distressed upon her account.

"Have you been long in London?" Virgie asked, wondering what caused the cloud upon his brow.

"Can you ask that?" he returned, with a look that made her own eyes droop. "I arrived this evening with my guardian, and, finding cards for Lady Huntington's reception, dropped in to pay my regards to the young ladies; but I could not be long in London without availing myself of the privilege that I craved when we parted. But," glancing around and realizing that their meeting was attracting more attention than was agreeable, "will you let me take you out for an ice? It is very warm here."

Virgie gladly availed herself of this invitation, for his sudden coming had agitated her, and she did not feel quite at her ease, while she, too, saw that her meeting with Rupert had excited considerable surprise in the group around her.

The young man led her to a small reception-room, found her a comfortable chair, and then remarked: "Now, if you will excuse me for a moment, I will get an ice for you."

"Please do not," Virgie interrupted, laying her hand lightly on his arm to detain him; "I do not care for it. I was only glad of an excuse to get away from the crowd for a few minutes' quiet chat with you——"

She stopped suddenly and colored with confusion at her confession; but Rupert, with a radiant glow on his face, drew a chair and sat down beside her.

"Thank you," he said; "and now tell me how have you enjoyed London during the last ten days."

"I am afraid my enjoyment of London has been rather doubtful," Virgie returned, laughing, "since I have seen scarcely anything of it for the fog and rain; but I have met a good many people whom I consider simply delightful."

"And, judging from the court you were holding when I came in to-night, those very people would return the compliment most heartily," said Rupert, smiling.

"Did your guardian accompany you this evening?" Virgie asked, by way of changing the subject.

"No; he was rather weary, and begged me to make his excuses to Lady Huntington."

"You have never told me who your guardian is, Mr. Hamilton."

"Haven't I? Then I have been very negligent, for he is the best friend I have in the world. He is Sir William Heath, and I hope to have an opportunity to introduce you to him soon."

"Do you intend to remain in London?" Virgie asked.

"For the present. Sir William Heath has a house in town, and we shall all be here for several weeks. By 'all' I mean Sir William's sister, Lady Linton, her daughter Lillian, who is a young lady a little older than yourself, and—your humble servant," explained Rupert.

"Lady Linton!" Virgie repeated, thoughtfully; "where have I heard that name before? It is very familiar, and yet I cannot recall the person to whom it belongs."

"Very likely you have heard it spoken in society here, as Lady Linton is in the habit of going out a good deal when in town," returned the young man.

"Perhaps so," Virgie assented, and yet almost positive she had heard it before ever coming to London.

They chatted a little longer, and then the young girl said she must return to the company, and Rupert, giving her his arm, conducted her back to the drawing-room.

But once there, she was again surrounded by a merry company, and he had no further opportunity to converse with her.

The next morning, however, he called at Mrs. Alexander's lodgings, and was very cordially received by that lady, whom he found looking far better than he had ever seen her.

She was rapidly regaining flesh and strength, and much of her old-time beauty as well. He had not realized until now how very lovely she was.

Virgie was not in when he arrived—she was out driving with the Misses Huntington, her mother told him—and, knowing that he could not long refrain from speaking of his love for the beautiful girl, he resolved that he would improve this opportunity and crave Mrs. Alexander's permission to address her daughter with the hope of winning her for his wife.

But how to broach the subject so near his heart was an embarrassing question, and after the first few moments he became thoughtful, and even pale, causing Mrs. Alexander to wonder if anything had gone wrong with him since his return.

"I am afraid your native air does not agree with you, Mr. Hamilton," said his hostess, breaking an awkward pause; "you are not looking as well as when I saw you last."

The truant color rushed into the young man's face in a torrent at this remark, and he made a bold venture, resolved to put his fate to the test at once.

"It is not my 'native air,' Mrs. Alexander," he answered, smiling slightly; "but, finding you alone this morning, I have been impelled to confess something to you, and yet I find myself lacking the courage to break the ice."

"Surely, I did not suppose that I was one to inspire fear in anyone," remarked his friend, archly.

"You are not; but when one's dearest hopes are at stake, it is sometimes hard to speak of them," Rupert answered, gravely; then added, frankly: "Mrs. Alexander, you must have suspected ere this how fondly I love your daughter. I have loved her ever since our meeting on that California trip last winter, and I have only been waiting for your sanction to my suit to open my heart to her. I hoped to see you last spring on my return to New York, but you had left the city and I could not learn your address. I then resolved to seek you again at the end of the summer, but you were still absent when I came back the last of September. You can, perhaps, imagine something of my disappointment—I may even say despair——when I found that I must return to England with no hope of confessing my love to Virgie. I do not need to tell you that I experienced a sudden ecstasy when I discovered that you were both on the same vessel with me and bound for the same port, and I could not have remained silent as long as I have, had it not been for the illness which kept my dear one a prisoner in her berth during our voyage. I know that I am, comparatively, a stranger to you, but you are so situated now that you can easily ascertain whether what I have to offer Virgie—a true heart, an untarnished name, and all that I have of this world's goods—is worthy of her acceptance. Mrs. Alexander, will you give me leave to try to win her?"

CHAPTER XIV.
THE BETROTHAL.

Mrs. Alexander smiled at the young lover's ardor, while she regarded his handsome, earnest face with a look almost of affection.

"Mr. Hamilton," she said, as he concluded, "to be frank with you, I must tell you that I have been expecting a request of this nature from you."

Rupert looked a trifle surprised at this declaration.

"A mother's eyes are very sharp," the lady resumed, "and it has not required much penetration to see that you were learning to regard my Virgie with more than friendly affection; besides, Mr. Knight told me of the conversation that he had with you at San Jose, and warned me of what I might expect when you returned to New York. And now I will confess to you freely that I was very much opposed to the idea of having Virgie become the wife of an Englishman. I had reason for the prejudice, which I will explain to you some other time; and I resolved you two should not meet again if I could help it. I did help it, as you know; that was the reason why I left New York so early; but only to be overreached by fate, which decreed that we should all come aboard at the same time. The moment Virgie introduced you to me, on board the Cephalonia, I felt that I was powerless, and so resigned myself to the inevitable. I must admit, however," Mrs. Alexander added, with a genial smile, "that I was disarmed of my prejudices before I had known you many hours, and as I became better acquainted with you, I could but acknowledge with Mr. Knight, who, by the way, is a strong champion in your favor, that I should be proud to give my daughter to so true a man; and so, Mr. Hamilton, you have my full and free permission to win my darling if you can, and——"

"Oh, thank you!" Rupert cried, seizing his companion's hand in his gratitude, his face luminous with joy; "you have made me the happiest man in London."

"I like to see young people happy," Mrs. Alexander replied, still smiling, but with a little sigh; "and I imagine it is safe to tell you I think you have no cause for fear. But now tell me something about yourself and your family; I should not like to make inquiries about you of other people."

"There is not very much to tell," Rupert said. "I am an orphan; my mother died when I was an infant; my father was a major in her majesty's service, and the only relatives I have living are an uncle and his family, by the name of Shaftonsbury, so my home has been with my guardian in Hampshire County——"

"Ah! Hampshire! Who is your guardian?" hastily asked Mrs. Alexander, paling a little at the familiar name.

"He was my father's dearest friend, Sir——" began Rupert, but before he could speak the name the door opened, and Virgie, looking flushed and beautiful from her exercise in the open air, stood upon the threshold, and the young man, forgetting both question and answer, sprang forward to greet her.

The conversation became general then for a little while; but by and by Mrs. Alexander excused herself, saying she had letters to write, and left the young couple alone.

Rupert's eyes had been seeing a great deal ever since Virgie came in; so much that she could not meet them without her color coming and going with tell-tale consciousness; and when, the moment the door closed after her mother, he arose and came to her side, she knew instinctively what was trembling on his lips.

"My darling," he said, in a low, earnest tone, "I have just told your mother that I love you, and she has given me leave to win you if I can. Virgie, I have loved you ever since those delightful days that we spent together on the way to California. I might have told you of it even then, had not Mr. Knight and my own sense of what was right warned me against it. But now, dearest, there are no barriers, unless you yourself raise one between us, and my heart bids me hope that you will not. Tell me, dear, that you love me—that you will be my wife."

He knelt by her side and gathered the two small hands that lay upon her lap into his, while he searched the lovely downcast face with his eager eyes.

She did not repulse him; she made no effort even to release her hands from his clasp. She cast one shy, sweet glance into his face, a little smile of love and joy trembled on her lips, while rosy blushes surged up to the waves of bright hair lying on her forehead, and Rupert needed no other answer to assure him of his heart's desire.

"You do love me, my darling!" he cried, drawing her into his arms. "I read it in your dear face, in your beautiful eyes; but let me hear it from your lips. I am selfish enough not to be satisfied with anything less. Virgie, you will give yourself to me?"

"Yes," she whispered, her head drooping until her hair almost mingled with his; "you *made* me love you on that journey."

"Oh, if I had known it then I fear I could not have held my peace," he interrupted, laying his lips fondly against her forehead. "I had, in fact, to run away from you at San Jose lest I should violate all bonds and betray myself in spite of the caution of Mr. Knight, who said I must wait until you were safely back with your mother."

"Did Mr. Knight suspect?" faltered Virgie, growing crimson again.

"Indeed he did. He is a very observing old gentleman, and took me to task for monopolizing you so much. He was right, too, dear, for it would have been rash and imprudent for me to have tried to win you then, and I honored him for restraining me, though it required a terrible wrench for me to tear myself away from you; but I knew my only safety was in flight. I resolved, however, that I would settle the question when I returned to New York; but I was very miserable when I came back in May and could not find you."

"And I, too, Rupert," Virgie confessed. "I thought it is very hard when the doctor ordered mamma away just at the very time when I was looking for you; but of course I could not say a word, for her health was of more importance than anything else, while——"

"While what, Virgie?" her lover asked, as she stopped in confusion.

"While I was not sure but that I was nourishing a delusion; and, taking it all in all, I was very wretched."

"Ah! and you have been loving me all this time?" Rupert breathed, as he bent to kiss the lips that had confessed so much. "And I have been fearing that you might send me away hopeless."

"I could not send you away, Rupert."

"Oh, Virgie, I hope I shall not wake to find this all a dream," he breathed, as he folded her closer in his arms, and drew her head upon his breast.

"Do not fear," the young girl returned, looking archly up into his eyes. "I assure you I have ample evidence that you are very much awake now, and, if you please, it won't do to disarrange my hair *too* much, for Grace Huntington is coming back in an hour to help me plan for Lady Dunforth's ball that is to occur next week."

Rupert laughed, but released her, smoothing very tenderly the tresses that he had disarranged; then seating himself on the sofa beside her, he asked:

"How will it be, my Virgie—can you be content to remain in England, or are you such a stanch American that you will pine for your native land?"

"It is said that 'home is where the heart is,' and if *you* are to live in England, I am afraid that America would not seem very home-like to me, even though it was my birthplace," Virgie confessed, with a shy smile that was very bewildering.

"Then you will not mind becoming an English matron?" Rupert observed, with a caress that again endangered the glossy tresses.

"Yes, I think I shall mind it very much," Virgie retorted; "so much that I should be unhappy to be anything else. Besides," she added, more gravely, "my father was an Englishman."

"Is it possible? But I do not think that Alexander is an English name," Rupert returned. "Of what portion of England was he a native?"

"I do not know, Rupert," Virgie said, looking troubled. "I imagine there is something about my father that mamma has never been willing to tell me. She always grows so sad and pale whenever I speak of him that I have not the heart to question her, although, as I have grown older, I have been very desirous of knowing more concerning him."

"Do you remember him?"

"Oh, no; I never saw him. He was called home to England a few weeks before my birth, and was lost."

"Lost at sea! How sad! Mrs. Alexander must have been very young."

"Yes, she was only a little over twenty."

"You will probably visit your father's home now that you are here," Rupert remarked.

"I asked mamma that one day, and she grew so white that I was frightened. She remarked that that was one object she had in coming abroad, but it was chiefly for my sake; and then she shivered as if there was something about it that she regarded with great dread. But hush! she is coming back to us."

Mrs. Alexander entered at that moment, and smiled as she saw the happy faces of the two young lovers, although Virgie was sure that there was a suspicious redness about her eyes, as if she had been weeping.

"I have won her, Mrs. Alexander," Rupert said, taking Virgie by the hand and leading her to her mother. "This dear girl has promised to be my wife, and I am sure you will give us your blessing and congratulations."

"Indeed I will," she responded, heartily, though she appeared greatly agitated as she drew Virgie into her arms and tenderly kissed her blushing cheek; "and I give her to you very willingly, because I feel sure that you are worthy of her, and I am confident that you will make each other happy. Still," she added, a little sadness in her voice, "it is not an easy thing for a mother to give away her only child, or to feel that she has been supplanted in her affections."

"Not supplanted, mamma—do not say that!" cried Virgie, clinging to her; "it could not be! I could never love you less, even though I——"

"Even though you love Rupert more," interposed her mother, archly. "I expect that, of course, and would not have it otherwise. I wish you to be all in all to each other, and," her voice growing husky with emotion, "may no cloud ever dim your happiness; may nothing ever come between you to mar your confidence in each other. Oh, my darling!" she cried, in a voice of agony, as she folded the lovely girl almost convulsively to her heart, and seeming to forget for the moment where she was, "I would rather lay you away in your grave to-day than to have you live to suffer what I have suffered."

"Mamma," cried Virgie, looking up anxiously into the almost convulsed face bending over her, "what can you mean? I have never seen you so unnerved before. Surely if you are in trouble, you should not hide it from me."

"Forgive me, love, for casting a shadow upon your joy at this time," said her mother, recovering herself with an effort; "but your happiness brought back all my own early hopes—hopes that were most cruelly blighted—so vividly that I forgot myself. Do not mind me, Virgie; your future looks very bright, and I have done wrong even to allude to anything to distress you on this day of all others."

Virgie stood back and looked gravely into her mother's face.

"Mamma," she said, with a seriousness that was new to her, "I fear that you have been hiding something from me all my life. I have often suspected it, and your excessive agitation this morning proves it. If you have known any great trouble in the past; if, as I surmise, it is connected with my father, I feel that you ought to confide it to me, and let me at least sympathize with, if I cannot alleviate, your sorrow."

Mrs. Alexander grew very thoughtful at these words. For a moment she stood irresolute, then a look of resolve overspread her face, and she said:

"Sit down, my children, and listen to me. I believe the time has come when I should open my heart to you, my Virgie, and since Rupert is now one of us it will be just as well for him to hear the story that I have to tell you at the same time; it will save a repetition, and I am not strong enough to review the past many times. Perhaps, too," she added, turning to the young man, who, in obedience to her request, had drawn his betrothed back to her seat upon the sofa, "you may be able to give me some advice regarding a duty which I have soon to perform."

She sat down near the lovers as she ceased speaking, but looking more like a statue of wax than a living being, for it seemed almost like going to her own execution to confess the wrongs which had been the death-blow to all the hopes of her own youth.

CHAPTER XV.
"I HAVE MET LADY LINTON BEFORE."

"You have always supposed, Virgie," Mrs. Alexander continued, after pausing a moment to summon all her fortitude for the duty which lay before her, "that your father was dead."

"And is he not, mamma?" cried the startled girl, growing almost as pale as her mother, and casting a terrified look upon her lover.

"No, dear; he is still living and here in England."

"Mamma!" and the cry of dismay, almost of agony, smote heavily on the fond mother's heart, while Rupert Hamilton gazed from one to the other, a look of wonder on his fine face.

"Be quiet, Virgie," returned Mrs. Alexander, gently. "No stigma rests upon either your name or mine, as I perceive you apprehend. Although I was most cruelly deserted in less than a year after my marriage, and at a time when I needed tenderest care and sympathy; although I was scorned and repudiated by the family of the man whom I had wedded; although I was left weak, unprotected, and comparatively destitute in a strange city—yet I have risen above it all; I have been able to prove that I was a lawful wife; that my child could claim an honored name, and it is for that purpose that I am here in London to-day. But let me begin at the beginning, and tell you all about it."

She went back to the commencement of her acquaintance with Sir William, although she did not call him by name—she was not quite ready to reveal that yet—and related all the story of his visit to that settlement among the mountains of Nevada. She told how he had won her; how kind he had been to her invalid father, and how they had been married while he was so ill; how, after his death, her husband had taken her to many places of interest in order to win her mind from her grief, and had made himself so necessary and was so devoted to her that she had grown to idolize him and to believe him the truest and noblest man on earth. She told of his sudden recall to England, while she was obliged to remain behind; of the sudden cessation of letters; of the arrival at the hotel, where she was boarding, of two English ladies, whom she did not name, who were the means finally of her discovering her husband's faithlessness, his previous engagement to one of his own countrywomen, and his subsequent marriage with her, in defiance of those bonds that he had assumed in connection with her. She related how she had at once returned to the West, where she had collected incontestable proofs of her marriage, notwithstanding that she had no certificate; how she had been enabled to turn her artistic talents to account and provide for her own necessities. She spoke of the divorce that she had obtained, and her reasons for wishing to secure it, scorning to remain bound to a man who had deserted her, and yet desirous of saving another pure woman from dishonor. Then she told something of her father's history and fortunes, of her uncle's return, his repentance and restitution, and the provision which he had made for her and which had placed her forever beyond the fear of want or the need of toil, even though she might never recover the fortune that her father had left her, or succeed in establishing Virgie's claim to her inheritance.

It was a sad, heart-breaking story, and told with thrilling power and earnestness by the long-tried woman, who almost seemed to be enduring again the sufferings of her early life; and when at length it was concluded, she was nearly exhausted by the effort it had cost her.

Virgie had long since crept to her mother's side, and was now in tears, with her arms twined about her and her head resting on her bosom; while Rupert sat near with averted eyes and looking grave and deeply distressed.

"Oh, mamma, why have you not told me this before?" Virgie at length asked, trying to control her sobs.

"Because, my darling, I could not bear to sadden your young life."

"But I could have sympathized with you, and then I need not have pained you by asking so many distressing questions."

"It was better for me to bear my burden alone," her mother persisted; "of course I know it would have to be told some time, but I have put it off as long as I could. Now, however, I must soon confront the man who has so wronged us, and demand justice and restitution for you, and so it has become necessary that you should know all this sad history."

"But, mamma, if he was married to that other woman there may be other children, and—and——"

Virgie could not go on, but broke down in distress.

"True; there are—at least I know of one; but that fact cannot affect your claim or deter me from demanding that you be recognized as the legitimate heir; for, of course, unless he made his second marriage legal, after the divorce was obtained, you alone have any lawful claim upon him," returned Mrs. Alexander, in a resolute tone, and with a look that denoted an inflexible purpose.

"But that will be dreadful," Virgie said, greatly troubled; "just think of the shame that such a proceeding would bring upon those who are innocent of wrong; they are not to blame for the evil that my—that their father has done, and it does not seem right that they should be made to suffer, or be deprived of their inheritance; think of their poor mother and all her hopes for her children."

"Does it count for nothing, Virgie, that my hopes were crushed; that I was abandoned when you were a helpless little one; that I was left to depend upon myself and to provide for you?" cried her mother, sternly; though there was a note of keenest agony in her tones. "Does it count for nothing that the happiness of my whole life has been wrecked; that I was repudiated, scorned, mocked; that you have never been acknowledged by your own name, never allowed to occupy your true position in life?"

"I know it has all been wrong, cruel, wicked," Virgie returned, sadly and with trembling lips; "but I have been very happy, with you, mamma; you have never allowed me to realize anything of this trouble; we have had everything we needed, and your fortune is ample without striving for that which you affirm should be mine; I cannot bear to think that anyone must be made to suffer just to secure a little more wealth, or a higher position in life, for me."

"And are you willing to sacrifice all your rights to those who have supplanted you—who have lived all their lives upon your heritage?" demanded Mrs. Alexander, excitedly.

"Mamma," Virgie answered, sitting up and meeting her mother's flashing eye with a proud look, "leaving the innocent out of the question entirely, I scorn to accept anything from the man who has so wronged you; I would not be recognized as his child; I would not be known by his name, were he allied to royalty itself."

Mrs. Alexander leaned forward and kissed the beautiful girl, clasping her fondly to her.

"Ah, my darling, you are not lacking in spirit, in spite of your forgiving nature," she said; "but justice demands that he shall make you restitution; that must be part of his punishment."

Then turning to Rupert she continued:

"You are a man, just and true, Mr. Hamilton; you have heard my story as a disinterested witness, and are therefore capable of judging with an unprejudiced mind; I ask you, is it right that I should demand for my child the position and inheritance that belong to her?"

And Rupert Hamilton replied, gravely, decidedly:

"It is right; a great wrong has been done both you and Virgie, and it is but just that it should be atoned for as far as may be—if not willingly, then by compulsion."

The young man little realized that he was passing sentence upon his respected and well-beloved guardian; but he had been greatly shocked by the story to which he had listened, and he deemed no punishment too severe for him who had been guilty of such wrong.

Virgie sighed at his verdict. She never could bear the thought of giving pain to others, and she shrank almost with loathing from meeting one who had caused her mother so much unhappiness.

"Mamma, who is my father?" she asked, after a thoughtful pause.

"My dear, I do not wish to tell you just yet, for you are liable to meet him or some members of his family in society, and you will be happier not to know it, at least until my plans are matured and I have decided when and how to act. I have simply related this story to you now because I thought that Rupert ought to know something of our history, and to prepare you for what must soon occur."

"Very well; I will wait your time," the young girl returned; but a little shiver of dread crept over her; she felt that she could never forgive or own the man who had so ill-treated her beautiful mother.

"And one thing more," continued Mrs. Alexander, turning to Rupert. "I should prefer that your engagement remain unannounced for a little while, until this business is settled. My lawyer hopes to be able to arrange matters in the course of two or three weeks."

"It shall be just as you wish," the young man responded, adding, with a fond smile, as he turned to Virgie: "So long as I am assured of the love that I crave it matters little to me whether the world knows it or not for the present. I would, however, like to make one exception. I should like to inform my guardian of the fact."

"That is but right," returned Mrs. Alexander; and she was again about to ask the name of his guardian, but a ring of their bell just then warned them that Miss Huntington had arrived, and as she entered Rupert took his leave, wondering to himself who this man was, who evidently stood so high in London society, and who had so ruthlessly ruined the life of a beautiful and trusting woman and discarded his own child.

A few evenings after this Virgie, accompanied by her mother for the first time, attended the reception and ball given by Lord and Lady Dunforth.

Lady Dunforth had herself been a beautiful American girl—Brownie Douglas by name—and she was always eager to entertain her countrywomen when they visited London.

She had met Virgie at the Huntingtons, and had at once been attracted toward her, and had taken pains to secure her presence on her next evening at home, arranging for extra attractions for her sake.

Mrs. Alexander was feeling unusually well on this night, and had taken a great deal of pains with her own and her daughter's toilet.

Virgie's costume was exquisite, consisting of pale blue satin, with an overdress of misty lace, wrought with tiny crystals, and draped with clusters of blush-roses, while she wore strings of rare pearls on her neck and arms and in her hair.

Mrs. Alexander wore simple black, but of richest material and finest texture, while her laces were exceptionally rare and her diamonds of the purest water.

She was a strikingly beautiful woman. Her form was finely developed, and yet it had lost nothing of the graceful outline of her maidenhood. Her face possessed a peculiar delicacy of beauty, and her complexion was as faultless as of old. She had gained much in ease and self-possession; her bearing was regal, her manner charming.

Lady Dunforth was even more delighted with her than she had been with Virgie, and took especial pains to present her to her most honored guests.

It happened that Lady Linton and Lillian were also present that evening.

Both were accomplished society women, and were much sought after, because of their tact and brilliancy, for there was never any lack of life, there was never any stiffness or awkwardness where they were. Lady Linton could entertain charmingly, and Lillian was always the center of a brilliant circle.

But for once Lady Linton's accomplishment in this direction failed her.

As Lady Dunforth was presenting Mrs. Alexander to some of her guests, she suddenly came face to face with Sir William Heath's sister.

"Ah! Lady Linton," said her hostess, in her genial way, "I have a friend here to whom I would like to introduce you; Mrs. Alexander—Lady Linton."

Her ladyship gave one glance into the beautiful face before her, and recognized it.

She knew her instantly for the woman who had saved her life at the time of that frightful railroad disaster eight years previously; who had nursed her so faithfully during the illness that followed, and who had afterward told her, "I am the woman whom your brother loved—whom he wooed and won."

A deadly pallor overspread her countenance, while her customary elegant self-possession was utterly routed. She was actually stricken dumb—her lips refused to pronounce the name she had heard, in acknowledgment of the introduction; she could only stand still with her eyes fastened in a blank, startled stare upon that graceful figure, while her heart sank a dead weight in her bosom.

Instinctively Lady Linton knew why Mrs. Alexander was there in London. She had come to fulfill the threat that she had uttered so long ago, and a terrible despair settled down upon the finished woman of the world, rendering her speechless, constrained, embarrassed.

Mrs. Alexander, however, was entirely at her ease. She had expected to meet this woman in society at some time or other, and was prepared for the encounter.

She bowed with exceeding grace, but with a suspicion of ironical politeness, while she remarked in cool, placid tones:

"I have had the pleasure of meeting Lady Linton before."

The sound of her voice broke the spell that held her ladyship enthralled; she managed to bow and to murmur some inarticulate words in return, then Lady Dunforth passed on with her guest, wondering if Lady Linton was ill, that she should appear so unlike herself.

CHAPTER XVI.
MORE INTRODUCTIONS.

Meanwhile another spiritual episode was transpiring in a different portion of Lady Dunforth's drawing-room.

Lillian Linton, brilliantly beautiful in pale pink silk, with elegant ornaments of opals, was entertaining a group of young people, while merry jest and sparkling repartee ran from lip to lip, when, chancing to glance toward the door, she saw Rupert Hamilton coming forward with a girl of bewildering loveliness leaning on his arm.

Her heart gave a great startled bound as she looked, for something in the glance, at once proud and fond, which the young man bent upon his fair companion—something in the happy, trustful eyes which Virgie raised to meet her lover's, told her that her own dream of love in connection with her uncle's ward could never be realized.

Rupert had appeared very different to her since his return from America. While he always treated her with every mark of politeness and friendliness, there was at the same time an unusual reserve—a constraint in his manner which seemed like a brazen wall between them.

At first she had told herself that it was because he had been absent so long; that when he was once more thoroughly settled at home matters would resume their usual course, and she would be able to win him by the witchery of her charms.

But he had been restless and absent-minded; he was anxious to get back to London, and could hardly control his impatience until the family completed their arrangements to go for a while to their town house.

Now she could understand it all. She was quick and keen enough to comprehend why his handsome face was all aglow; why his eyes beamed with that tender, unaccustomed light that called the soft color to the young girl's cheeks and wreathed her red lips with happy smiles—he loved and was beloved.

Her proud, passionate heart instantly arose in rebellion against the cruel fate which decreed that the sweetest hopes of her life must be blighted; that the love of which she had dreamed all her life, and which had grown into her soul so strong and deep, must be denied her, just as she had begun to feel so sure of winning it.

That the girl was peerlessly beautiful, and of a more delicate and refined type than herself, she realized with a pang of jealousy, and she was conscious, too, that Rupert was bringing her straight toward her, doubtless with the intention of introducing her.

Unlike her mother, she had a moment in which to compose and brace herself before meeting her rival; and, calling all her pride to her aid, she looked the picture of brilliant, happy maidenhood when Rupert reached her side.

"Lillian," he said, "I wish to introduce you to a friend; Miss Alexander—Miss Linton."

Lillian put forth her daintily gloved hand without a tremor, and, with a dazzling smile, expressed her pleasure at making her acquaintance.

"Miss Alexander is an American," Rupert explained, and Lillian's heart sank; a sudden faintness seemed to come over her at his words.

Her brother Percy's prophecy had been verified; he had fallen in love with this girl while on his tour in the United States.

But she would rather have died than betrayed anything of her dismay before the girl, and looking straight into Virgie's clear eyes, she said, brightly:

"Ah! then I suppose you have recently come abroad, as I have not met you before."

"Yes, we were passengers on the same steamer with Mr. Hamilton," Virgie answered, "and we owe him a great deal, for he was very kind to us—mamma and me."

"And how do you like England and English people?"

"Very much," Virgie replied, smiling, while her eyes turned instinctively to Rupert, as if she judged the whole nation by her estimate of him.

Lillian shut her white teeth together viciously as she saw the look and Rupert's answering smile, and she wondered what her mother would say when she learned that her uncle's ward had bestowed his heart upon a hated American.

"Have you ever been in the United States, Miss Linton?" Virgie asked, wholly unconscious of the disturbance which her presence was creating.

"Yes, I traveled considerably there one summer several years ago."

"And were you pleased with my country?"

"Well, of course America is very different from England, and I like my own land best, although America has some grand scenery," Lillian responded. "But mamma came near losing her life there in a terrible railway accident, and I was only too glad to get safely home again."

"Oh!" said Virgie, with a quick indrawn breath, "I remember; we were on that very train. Is that Lady Linton your mother?"

"Yes; how strange that you should have been in that accident, too?" returned Lillian, greatly surprised. "Were you injured?"

"No; mamma and I both escaped unhurt, though my maid had one arm badly broken. I can just remember Lady Linton; mamma took me to see her just before we left the place; I was sure I had heard the name before, when Mr. Hamilton mentioned her to me one day last week, but I could not place it."

"I wonder——" began Lillian, excitedly, and then she suddenly checked herself.

She was just upon the point of saying, "I wonder if your mother was the lady who was so kind to mamma while she was so ill."

Lady Linton had been obliged to confirm her physician's statements to her son when he arrived, that a brave woman had saved her life at the time of the accident, and then carefully and faithfully nursed her through a critical crisis afterward; but she pretended not to know her name and never mentioned her again, though Percy and his sister often spoke of the circumstance with considerable curiosity and interest.

Virgie raised questioning eyes, as Lillian cut herself short, and she felt compelled to complete her sentence in some way, so she said:

"I wonder there were not more lives lost at that time; it must have been a shocking accident. But have you seen Lady Dunforth's Japanese curiosities, Miss Alexander?"

"No, I have not," Virgie answered, thinking her new acquaintance had changed the subject rather abruptly.

"Then let me take you to examine them, Vir—Miss Alexander," Rupert interposed, eagerly, glad of an excuse to get her again to himself, and Virgie, bowing a graceful adieu to Lillian, took his arm and allowed him to lead her from the room.

Lillian watched them with an angry, aching heart, but she was obliged to conceal her feelings, for she knew that others were observing her, and not for the world would she have her jealous fears suspected; so it was not long before she was again the life and center of an admiring circle.

Rupert led Virgie to a small room opposite the drawing-room, which had been fitted up in Japanese style, and where many curiosities and choice bric-a-brac from that country had been collected and tastefully arranged.

It was a lovely room, and Virgie was delighted with its unique treasures.

The lovers spent some time examining the different objects and in the enjoyment of each other's society, and they had nearly made the round of the room when someone put aside the curtains of the door-way and entered.

Rupert glanced up, and then started forward, his face lighting with a smile of pleasure.

"Uncle Will," he cried, "I did not know that you were coming here to-night. When did you arrive?"

"Only a few moments ago," returned Sir William Heath, regarding his ward affectionately. "I did not expect that I should be able to accept Lady Dunforth's invitation; in fact, I told Miriam I could not, but I managed to get through my business somewhat earlier than usual, and so concluded to drop in here for a little relaxation."

"I am glad you did; you are working too hard, Uncle Will, and need more recreation. But come, I have a friend here whom I want you to know," Rupert concluded, linking his arm within his guardian's and leading him toward Virgie, who was examining an elaborate piece of embroidery on the opposite side of the room.

"Ah! a young lady!" remarked Sir William, archly, as his glance fell upon the pretty figure; her face he could not see, for it was turned from him.

Rupert colored slightly at his tone, but he said nothing until he reached the side of his betrothed, then he remarked:

"Miss Alexander, I want to introduce you to the best friend I have in the world, my guardian, Sir William Heath."

Virgie turned, a smile of pleasure on her lips, for she had longed to meet Rupert's guardian, and something in the fair face which she lifted to him, in that delicate profile, in those refined features, in the glancing of her eye, and in the very movement she made, as she stepped forward to greet him, suddenly smote the baronet with the strangest sensation that he ever experienced, yet he never dreamed that he was looking into the face of his own daughter!

It almost seemed to him as if he had known her before in some previous state of existence—as if somewhere in the dim and misty past their souls had met and held sweet and genial converse.

For a moment he hardly knew whether he was in the body or out; a mist obscured his sight, a mighty ringing was in his ears, dulling every other sound, while the very earth seemed quaking beneath his feet.

"Uncle Will, you are ill!" was the startled remark that recalled him to himself, and made him suddenly realize that he was conducting himself very strangely.

"No, my boy, it is only a sudden dizziness; it will pass in a moment; it is gone even now, and I beg pardon for alarming you and your friend," the baronet replied, as his vision began to clear and he met the beautiful dark eyes of the young girl fixed upon him with a look of deep concern.

He put out a hand to steady himself, even as he spoke, and she took a step forward, drawn toward him by a power of attraction she could not understand.

"Pray sit down, Sir William; have this rocker," she said, as she drew forward a light but roomy willow chair for him.

"Thanks," he returned; "let us all sit; we can chat a few moments more comfortably so," and he gladly sank into the rocker, still feeling as if the floor was slipping from under him.

Rupert drew another chair for Virgie, and then went to get a glass of water for his guardian, for his pallor alarmed him greatly.

But he was soon entirely himself again, making light of his sudden attack, and they sat and talked some time about the curiosities around them.

But the baronet watched every movement of the fair young stranger with an eager, wistful eye. Her grace charmed him more and more; even the tones of her voice thrilled him with a painfully sweet sensation, and whenever she addressed him the tears would almost start into his eyes.

"Are you a stranger in London?" he asked, after a little pause in their conversation.

"Yes, sir; but I have not been allowed to remember the fact since coming here—everyone is so kind," she said, smiling.

"Where is your home?" he inquired.

"In New York city, on the other side of the Atlantic."

"Indeed! Then you have come hither recently?"

"It is scarcely three weeks since my arrival in London," Virgie returned.

Sir William turned a questioning look upon Rupert.

"I met Miss Alexander during my trip, Uncle Will," he said, quietly, but coloring beneath his glance.

"Alexander!" repeated the baronet, with a sudden start.

"I did not quite catch the name before. Is New York your parents' native place?"

"No, sir. Mamma's early home was in the West, and my father—oh! what have I done?"

In her nervousness, caused by speaking of her father, Virgie had swept something from the table, by which she was sitting, with a motion of her arm, and it had fallen with a crash to the floor.

"No harm," Rupert returned, as he stooped to pick it up, "it is only a metallic paper knife and could not break. It is, however, a curiously carved affair; had you noticed it?" and he passed it to her to examine, for he observed that she was disturbed and excited by the mention of her father.

Virgie took it, glad of an excuse for changing the subject, and then they all fell to discussing the skill and ingenuity of the Japanese.

While they sat thus, a face suddenly looked in upon them from the hall.

It was the face of Lady Linton.

She had heard voices there, while passing, and stepped to the door-way, impelled by an unusual curiosity.

She took in the situation instantly.

Her brother had told her that he could not attend Lady Dunforth's reception that evening, and, ever since her encounter with Mrs. Alexander, she had been congratulating herself that he had been detained, while now she had found him here, sitting face to face with his own daughter, and perhaps upon the very verge of discovering her relationship to him.

She could have shrieked aloud with terror and anger.

Must all her skillfully wrought plans come to naught?

Had she sacrificed truth and honor for years, to fail now—to have the woman whom she had hated all her life triumph over her at last?

No! She would fight it out to the bitter end; if there was any power on earth that could keep them apart they should never meet, and she must begin now—this instant, by breaking up this interesting group.

"William!" she cried, in a strangely altered voice, "*you here!*"

Sir William started up at the words, turned and saw his sister standing upon the threshold with a face of ghastly whiteness.

"Yes. What is the matter, Miriam?" and he sprang forward and caught her in his arms, just as she was falling to the floor in a well-feigned swoon.

CHAPTER XVII.
SOME STARTLING DISCOVERIES.

Of course the attention of all centered at once upon Lady Linton, and Sir William's interest in his beautiful but unknown daughter was, for the time, merged in his anxiety for his sister.

As it happened, there was no one else in the room just then, and Rupert and his guardian laid the apparently unconscious woman upon a lounge that was standing near, and immediately exerted themselves for her recovery.

Virgie, too, was very helpful, dipping her own dainty handkerchief into some water that Rupert brought, and bathing Lady Linton's face with it, while she gave directions to Sir William about chafing her hands to assist in restoring circulation.

When the woman began to show signs of recovery and opened her eyes, she found herself looking directly into the face of the lovely girl whose presence there had caused her so much concern.

"Where is my brother?" she demanded, jerking her head away from the gentle hand that was ministering so tenderly to her.

"I am here, Miriam," said Sir William, bending over her. "What shall I do for you?"

"Take me home," she replied, with a shiver, as she glanced darkly at Virgie, who had drawn back and was standing beside Rupert.

"I will, as soon as you are able," her brother replied.

"I am able now," and she sat up with surprising energy for one who but a few moments before had appeared so seriously ill.

"Very well; I will attend you immediately," Sir William responded; "but," he added, as he regarded her anxiously, "what could have caused this sudden attack? I never knew you to faint before."

A guilty stain shot for a moment into Lady Linton's cheeks.

"I imagine the rooms are overheated, and I have not been quite myself this evening," she said, which was true enough, for there had been a deadly sinking at her heart ever since her encounter with her brother's former wife.

She glanced uneasily toward the door as she spoke, for she was in mortal terror lest she should chance to make her appearance there in search of her daughter, and she felt that she would rather drop dead, there at her brother's feet, than to have those two, so long parted by her plotting, meet and become reconciled.

Her purpose now was to get him out of that house and away from London as soon as possible, and she resolved to stop at nothing to accomplish her object. It was a terrible blow to her to find that woman there. So many years had elapsed, during which she had kept silence, that she had grown to feel very secure in her position as mistress of her brother's home, and she had fully expected that she would retain it as long as she should live, and had come to regard the threats which the injured wife had made in the past as so many idle words.

Life of late had looked brighter to her than at any previous time since her marriage. Percy had recently become engaged to a beautiful girl—one in every way worthy of him, and who, when she became his wife, would bring with her a noble dower; indeed, her father was so much pleased with his prospective son-in-law that he had himself proposed to relieve Linton Grange of all incumbrances, and thus all the burden entailed by his father's profligacy would be lifted from the young lord's shoulders.

Lillian's *début* in society had been very brilliant; she was greatly admired and much sought after; so the mother's cup of pride and joy in her children seemed to be full to the brim.

The only bitter drop in it was Lillian's unrequited affection for Rupert, and Lady Linton had never relinquished the hope of succeeding in accomplishing even this marriage until after the young man's return from America.

He had seemed very different since then; restless and preoccupied, but betraying at the same time an undercurrent of joy which told of some sweet hope cherished in his heart, the fulfillment of which he was eagerly awaiting.

His treatment of Lillian was courteous and respectful, but not calculated to inspire anyone with the belief that he regarded her with feelings of more than ordinary friendship, and thus Lady Linton had begun to fear that her favorite and his magnificent fortune were likely to slip from her grasp and become the prey of some more fortunate beauty and belle.

She had not, however, had a suspicion of *who* was to be the favored maiden, until she came so suddenly upon that group in the Japanese parlor, when she had taken in at a glance the mortifying and exasperating truth, and immediately she was wrought almost into a frenzy between anger and fear, and ready to adopt the most daring measures to protect herself from exposure.

But to return to the Japanese parlor.

Lady Linton arose as she replied to her brother's questions, and signified her readiness to leave immediately.

"Wait a moment here," he said, "while I go to make our excuses to Lady Dunforth and tell Lillian that we are going."

"No—oh, do not leave me, William!" pleaded Lady Linton, growing frightfully pale again and trembling visibly; she would not trust him one moment in that drawing-room, lest he should meet Virginia Alexander. "I am afraid I shall have another fainting turn. Let Rupert see her ladyship. Will you?" she asked, turning to him.

"Certainly," he answered, readily.

"Thank you. And now, William, if you will please ring for a servant to bring my wraps here. I do not feel equal to the effort of going for them."

Sir William did as she requested, wondering to see her so unnerved. Nothing had ever seemed to unsettle her like this before.

"And, Rupert," she continued, "won't you be so good as to look after Lillian for the rest of the evening, and see that she gets home safely?"

"I will do anything you wish," the young man returned, although he was not very well pleased with this latter commission, for he had anticipated a pleasant drive and chat with Virgie, as it had been his intention to attend her home.

"I do particularly wish this," Lady Linton said, with decision. "It would not be proper for Lillian to come by herself, and I do not quite like to alarm her or tear her away so early while she is enjoying herself so much. Ah! here come my wraps," she concluded, with a sigh of relief, as a servant appeared with them.

She put them on with nervous haste, and then turning to her brother, said, almost peremptorily:

"Come, William, I am ready."

"In one moment, Miriam."

He had stepped back and was standing before Virgie, who, keenly sensitive regarding Lady Linton's evident aversion to her, had withdrawn herself from her immediate presence.

He held out his hand to her, saying, as he smiled almost tenderly down on her upturned face:

"It has been a great pleasure to me to meet you. I trust we shall see each other again soon."

"I think you will, Uncle Will," Rupert interposed, in a tone that made his guardian turn and regard him searchingly, while he said to himself:

"I do believe the young scamp is in love with her. I would not wish a more charming little wife for him, but I am afraid it will be rather hard on Lillian."

"Thank you, Sir William," Virgie returned, and there was a slight tremor in her voice, for the presence of this man thrilled her strangely. "I am sure the pleasure has been mutual, and I should feel very sorry if I thought I should not meet you again."

"William!" interrupted his sister, impatiently; and giving the soft hand he was holding a last, lingering pressure, the baronet turned away, with a sigh, and attended his sister to her carriage, while Rupert took Virgie to the drawing-room, where he sought Lillian, to inform her of her mother's sudden indisposition and departure.

An hour later Mrs. Alexander and Virgie retired, for the former was not strong yet, and therefore unequal to very much dissipation.

Rupert attended them to their carriage, but just as they were about to enter it an elegant coupe drew up beside it, and Mrs. Alexander's attention was instantly attracted by a device that was emblazoned upon one of its panels.

She stopped with her foot upon the step, and turned for a nearer view.

A startled, surprised look came into her face.

The coat of arms represented a patriarchal cross, while underneath it there were stamped the words, "*Droit et Loyal.*"

"Whose carriage is that?" Mrs. Alexander asked of Rupert.

He glanced in the direction indicated.

"That is Lady Linton's," he replied; "she has sent it back for Lillian."

"Lady Linton's!" repeated Mrs. Alexander, with a start, while she thought it a little strange that he should speak so familiarly of her daughter and be so well informed of the lady's movements.

"Yes; Sir William Heath, her brother, presented both carriage and horses to her for her individual use one Christmas," Rupert explained.

"And what is that device upon the panel of the carriage door?"

"It is the Linton coat of arms."

"The Linton coat of arms! You seem to know the family well, Mr. Hamilton."

"And why should I not?" Rupert returned, smiling. "I have made my home with them during the last ten or twelve years. William Heath is my guardian."

"What?" cried his listener, sharply.

"Have I not told you before?" Rupert asked, looking up in surprise at her tone. "You must pardon me, Mrs. Alexander, for being so negligent; but surely, I thought I had informed you of the fact."

Mrs. Alexander clutched at the carriage door for support, and for a moment thought she must fall to the ground; two such startling discoveries as she had just made were sufficient to make her heart stand still and her blood run cold, and she scarcely had strength to move.

Rupert Hamilton Sir William Heath's ward?

It was a strange fate that had decreed that her daughter and his should become the *fiancée* of the young man he had reared.

She was aghast; her brain reeled and she stumbled into the carriage and sank weakly upon the seat, anxious to be gone, to be alone, and think it all out by herself.

Her face was deathly in its paleness, and Rupert, though he wondered at her strange behavior, so at variance with her usual courtesy, feared that she was displeased with him for his negligence.

"Am I forgiven?" he asked, smilingly, as he leaned in to tuck the robes about them.

His question brought the stricken woman somewhat to herself, and she replied:

"There is nothing to forgive, Mr. Hamilton. Of course, it was an oversight, your not mentioning that Sir William Heath was your guardian. Did Virgie know?"

"Yes, mamma. Rupert introduced me to him to-night as his best friend; but he had told me before, and I thought you knew," said the young girl, marveling at her mother's strange emotion.

"*Introduced him to you to-night! Was he here?*" cried the woman, with a gasp and a sense of suffocation.

"Yes. But, mamma, how strangely you act! Are you ill?" Virgie inquired, noticing, with increasing alarm, her mother's pale face and uncontrollable agitation.

"No—yes. Let me get home as soon as we can—I believe I am not well," and she sank weakly back among the cushions, almost panting for breath.

"Shall I come, too? Will you need me?" Rupert asked, anxiously.

"No, thank you," Mrs. Alexander answered, with a great effort. "It is not far—we shall soon be there—good-night!"

The young man would gladly have gone, but her tone was decisive, and he turned back into the mansion, as the carriage drove away, greatly puzzled by her strange manner, and at the way she had spoken of his guardian.

Mrs. Alexander scarcely spoke all the way home, and insisted upon going directly to her room alone, although Virgie begged to be allowed to do something for her—to stay with her during the night.

"All that I need is rest and quiet," she said. "Good-night my darling!"

She kissed her tenderly, wondering, with a terrible heart-pang, how she could ever tell her that her lover's guardian was her own father—the man who had so cruelly wronged his wife and child more than eighteen years ago.

Once in the room, without even stopping to remove her wraps, she went to her writing-desk, drew forth a package from a drawer in it, and took it to the light for examination.

It was the mysterious package which her uncle, Mark Alexander, had confided to her on his death-bed, charging her to return it to the owner should she ever discover who that person was.

She had discovered that night to whom it belonged.

She held the seal close to the candle, and gazed upon it with darkening eyes and sternly compressed lips. It was stamped with a shield bearing a patriarchal cross, and under it was the motto, *"Droit et Loyal."*

"How strange!" she murmured. "It belongs to his sister—to that woman who mocked and scorned me; whom I saved from a dreadful death, and nursed through a critical illness! She must have been one of those women whom Uncle Mark heard conversing together that day in the hotel parlor here in London. How wonderful that anything belonging to her should have fallen into my hands! How wonderful everything is—Virgie's betrothal to Rupert—her meeting with him to-night! How will it all end? To think that he was there, in the same house with me, this evening! I am really curious to know what this contains," she continued, turning the package over and over, and regarding it with troubled eyes, while her thoughts were busy with the past.

"Well," she concluded, after musing for several minutes, "it must be returned to its owner, I suppose. I promised, and I must fulfill my word. Yes," lifting her head resolutely, "she shall have it on the day that my darling stands within her ancestral halls the acknowledged heiress of Heathdale, not before."

CHAPTER XVIII.
A SUDDEN FLITTING.

The next morning Mrs. Alexander's lawyer, Mr. Thurston, made a call upon his client, and had an interview with her of more than two hours' duration.

After his departure, she sought Virgie, with a very grave face, and explained the nature of his business, which caused the young girl to open wide her lovely eyes and exclaim, with astonishment:

"Why, mamma, it is the strangest romance in the world! I never heard anything like it!"

"Well, dear, get yourself ready as soon as possible, for we must leave town this afternoon, as there is no time to lose," her mother replied, as she arose to go to make her own preparations for the proposed journey.

"But, mamma, what shall I do about Rupert?" Virgie asked, looking troubled.

Mrs. Alexander's face fell at the mention of the young man's name.

She had scarcely slept during the previous night, for many things troubled her, and, among others, the thought that Virgie's engagement to Rupert Hamilton seemed likely to complicate matters very much when she should be ready to make her claim upon Sir William Heath.

"You can leave a note telling him that we are obliged to leave town for a while, and we can explain further to him when we ascertain just how we are to be situated," her mother replied, after considering a moment.

So, when Rupert called that evening, he found only a note awaiting him instead of the bright face he had hoped to see, while it told him that his betrothed and her mother had been unexpectedly called away from London upon important business, which might detain them a week, perhaps longer.

"It is very strange that she does not mention where they are going," he said, as he read the note over for the second time, and remarked this omission. "Mrs. Alexander acted very strangely last evening. I wonder if this sudden departure can have had anything to do with that?"

He retraced his steps, feeling unaccountably depressed over the absence of Virgie, and he resolved to seek an interview with Sir William and acquaint him with the fact of his engagement that very evening.

He did not, however, find his guardian upon his return; he had gone out upon a matter of business, his valet told the young man, and would not be back until late; so he retired, resolving to improve the first opportunity on the morrow.

The next morning, after breakfast, he said, in a quiet aside:

"Can I have a few moments' conversation with you, Uncle Will?"

"Certainly, my boy. Come into the library in about ten minutes, and I will be there."

Lady Linton, always on the alert for everything of a mysterious nature, and doubly keen now to suspect mischief, heard this request, and at once resolved to become acquainted with the nature of the interview.

Sir William's chamber was just back of the library, although there was no door communicating with it.

The same furnace-pipe, however, conducted heat to the two rooms, and, by stationing herself close to this, her ladyship knew she could overhear whatever might pass between the two men. She therefore slipped quietly into her brother's bed-room, locked the door, and, creeping close to the register, laid her eager ear against it.

Rupert was already with Sir William, for the housekeeper had detained Lady Linton for a few moments with questions regarding some domestic matter, but she was in season to hear him broach the subject so near his heart.

"I have come to make a confession to you, Uncle Will," he said, as he seated himself opposite his guardian.

"A confession! Nothing very serious, I hope," said Sir William, glancing keenly into the flushed face of his ward.

"Yes, I think it is of rather a serious nature," he returned, smiling slightly. "I wish to tell you that I have become deeply attached to Miss Alexander, to whom I introduced you last night, and to ask your sanction to our engagement."

"Aha! has it gone so far as that?" inquired Sir William. "I began to surmise last evening that she was taking your heart captive, but did not imagine matters had reached a crisis yet."

"Don't you think her lovely, Uncle Will?" Rupert asked, eagerly.

"Very lovely; but, my boy, the ocean rolls between England and America. I cannot bear the thought of a separation from you, Rupert."

"Nor I from you, my dear guardian; and, I assure you, you need not fear it, for the young lady does not object to a permanent residence in England. I trust you will not oppose my marriage with Miss Alexander."

"Rupert," said Sir William, gravely, "my only wish is for your happiness, and if Miss Alexander is the woman of your choice—if you are sure that she alone can make you happy—then I can only say Heaven bless you and grant that your future may be all that you desire."

"Thank you, Uncle Will, I—I hope you do not disapprove of my choice of a wife?" Rupert said, regarding his guardian's grave face anxiously.

"No, no," returned the baronet, hastily. "I admired the little lady very much during the few moments that I spent with her last evening. She seems a lovely girl. My first thought was that she might take you from us."

"No. Although she was born in America, she is herself of English decent on her father's side, and she and her mother are now in this country, for the purpose of claiming some property inherited from him," Rupert explained.

"Ah! then she has no father."

"No; he—she—lost him when she was a child."

The young man began to fear he was trespassing somewhat upon Mrs. Alexander's confidence, and resolved that he would betray no more at present.

"Are you sure that the family is one with which you will feel proud to ally yourself?" Sir William inquired.

"I know but very little concerning their family," Rupert admitted. "I doubt if they have any, but everything about them indicates that they are above reproach, while Mr. Knight, the gentleman whom I met in America, and of whom you have often heard me speak, introduced them, and he is of irreproachable character. He occupies a high position in New York, and it is in compliance with his request that they are presented here, and chaperoned by the Huntingtons."

"The Huntingtons are all right, and would introduce no one regarding whom there was any question," Sir William said, in a satisfied tone. "Is Mrs. Alexander as much of a beauty as her daughter?" he concluded, smilingly.

"Hardly in my eyes," returned the young man, with heightened color; "and yet she is a remarkably handsome woman. I hope I may be able to arrange for you to make their acquaintance very soon; but until then please regard what I have told you as strictly confidential."

"Ah! Then you do not intend to announce your engagement just yet," remarked Sir William, with some surprise.

"No, sir. At Mrs. Alexander's request, we shall delay it for the present, until she secures the property of which I have already spoken."

"How much of an heiress is your pretty *fiancée* going to be, Rupert?" his guardian asked.

"I cannot tell. I do not even know of what this property consists," the young man answered, thoughtfully.

"I am afraid there is something a little mysterious about these ladies. Doesn't it strike you so?" inquired Sir William, gravely, yet without a suspicion of the wonderful truth.

Rupert knew there was, but he was not going to confess it, and he replied, evasively:

"I do not imagine there is anything but what will soon be satisfactorily explained to us all."

Lady Linton, hearing all this, and knowing so much more than either Rupert or her brother, grew deadly faint as she listened and realized how near she stood to the verge of a terrible exposure.

Just then there came a brisk tap on the library door, and the next moment Lillian put her bright face into the room, and looking as lovely as the morning itself in her white flannel wrapper, fastened at the waist with cherry ribbons, and with her hands full of jacqueminot roses.

Her face assumed a look of surprise as she saw Rupert there, and she regarded him with searching curiosity.

"Pardon me, Uncle Will," she said, flushing; "I did not know that you were engaged with anyone; I have just received a box of flowers, and came to arrange some for your table. May I come in? I won't be long."

"Yes, indeed, come in; you are doubly welcome coming with so much beauty and fragrance," said her uncle, smiling.

Rupert arose as she entered, and asked with an arch smile:

"What enamored swain has been guilty of the extravagance of lavishing such costly flowers upon you, Lillian?"

"Lord Ernest Rathburn is the donor; he has exquisite taste. I wish you could have seen the box when it came," the girl replied, with a conscious drooping of her brilliant eyes.

"Lord Ernest Rathburn!" repeated Rupert in a peculiar tone, which brought the angry color to Lillian's cheek.

Lord Ernest was a young nobleman with a large revenue, but possessing far less brains than mustache, and who was regarded with contempt by all manly young men, on account of his effeminacy and excesses.

"I wish," he added, "that you could meet a friend of mine, Lillian; you will, I hope, before very long. Lord Ernest would sink into insignificance by comparison."

"And who may this paragon of manly excellence be, Mr. Hamilton, if I may inquire?" Lillian asked, with a toss of her head.

"Harry Webster, the young man with whom I traveled, last winter, in America."

"I despise Americans," retorted Miss Linton, with considerable asperity.

"That is rather a sweeping assertion; isn't it, my dear?" asked Sir William, looking a trifle amused.

"It is the truth, Uncle Will, whatever else it may be," she retorted, as she began to arrange her flowers in a vase on the table. "I am English to the backbone. I am thoroughly imbued with a love for my own people, and I shall never permit myself to draw disloyal comparisons."

Rupert laughed outright as, in his mind, he placed the stooping figure and imbecile face of the halfwitted young lord beside the grandly developed form and frank, handsome countenance of his American friend.

"If you could place the two men side by side, I warrant you would be compelled to draw disloyal comparisons, in spite of your very praiseworthy patriotism, my fair cousin," he said, a roguish twinkle in his eyes.

Lillian shot an angry glance at those last words; nothing annoyed her more than to be called "sister" or "cousin" by Rupert.

"I thank you for acknowledging that I am imbued with patriotism. I wonder what has become of yours," she said, sarcastically.

"I have plenty of it, only I do not allow it to warp my judgment; I can appreciate both beauty and goodness whenever I find it, at home or abroad."

"That is a self-evident fact," remarked the young girl, dryly, and Rupert colored consciously.

"I give you credit for just as nice discrimination," he retorted. "Wait till you see my friend, Webster, and if he doesn't take the palm I shall 'lose my guess,' as the Yankees say."

"That is American slang; they are all insufferably coarse," Lillian returned, contemptuously.

"Did you meet the pretty little American, Miss Alexander, at Lady Dunforth's the other evening, Lillian?" inquired Sir William.

"Yes, I met her," the girl admitted, rather ungraciously.

"Well, you would hardly class her among those whom you term coarse, would you? I thought her an unusually attractive girl."

"No; I admit she appeared very pretty and lady-like and yet I have no doubt that she would soon betray her nationality if one was to see much of her."

"Neither have I; and she would be proud to own it, also, I'll wager," Rupert observed, with some spirit.

He was out of patience with Lillian's unreasonable prejudices, and her slighting tone in speaking of Virgie made him indignant.

She looked at him with a mocking smile on her red lips.

"When shall we have the pleasure of congratulating you upon your American conquest?" she asked, saucily.

"I shall take great pleasure in informing you when the proper time arrives," he replied, with studied politeness, and with a seriousness that drove all color from the girl's face and made her heart sink like lead in her bosom.

At that moment the butler entered the room with a telegram, which he presented to Sir William, and then withdrew.

The baronet tore it open and read:

"Come to Middlewich at once. William has had a dangerous fall.

MARGARET HEATH."

Middlewich was the country seat of the nobleman to whom the baronet's cousin, William Heath, was private secretary, and it was to this place that he was now so peremptorily summoned.

Lady Linton, in her hiding place, heard her brother read this telegram with a thrill of joy.

She was glad of anything that would take him out of London and away from the danger of meeting "that woman," and she resolved that it should go hard with her if she could not find some way of opposing other barriers before his return. It was a desperate case, and she was prepared for desperate measures.

She crept out of her brother's chamber with a pale, drawn face, saying to herself that Rupert Hamilton should never fulfill his engagement with Virgie Alexander, if there was any power on earth to prevent it; she could never bear the humiliation of it.

She packed her brother's portmanteau with alacrity, and promised to attend faithfully to his various commissions during his absence, and uttered a sigh of relief when the carriage drove from the door, and she knew that he was well on his way to Middlewich.

CHAPTER XIX.
AN UNEXPECTED MEETING.

Three days later Lady Linton received a letter from her brother, giving the particulars of his cousin's accident. He had been riding from Chester to Middlewich, when his horse became frightened at some object by the roadside, and Mr. Heath, not being sufficiently on his guard, had been thrown, suffering the fracture of two ribs, a broken arm, and, it was feared, some internal injury besides. He was in a very critical state at the time of Sir William's writing, and the latter said he should not think of returning to London until assured that his kinsman was out of danger.

"Thank fortune!" Lady Linton breathed, most fervently. "Of course," she added, a guilty flush rising to her forehead as she suddenly realized how heartless her expression sounded, "of course, I do not mean that I am thankful to have Cousin William suffer such injuries, but I am immeasurably relieved to have my brother called away just at this time, and the longer he stays, the better I shall be pleased."

She heard nothing more for a week, when there came another letter stating that Mr. Heath was slightly improved, but still unable to be moved, and quite a sufferer. There were some more particulars, too, regarding the accident.

Lord Norton, an aged friend of the Duke of Falmouth—the nobleman to whom Mr. Heath was private secretary—was very ill, and he had sent for his grace to confide to him a historical work upon which he had been engaged for more than two years. It was nearly completed, only a few more chapters to be copied, and Lord Norton, feeling that he should not live to see it published, desired his friend to take charge of it, finish it, and secure its publication.

The duke readily consented to put the work through; but, as his eyesight would not permit him to do very much in the way of either reading or writing, he suggested that his secretary, Mr. Heath, who was eminently qualified, should get it ready for press, and he himself would attend to its publication.

Lord Norton was pleased with this proposition, and Mr. Heath consented to take hold of the book at once, hoping to complete the copying while his lordship's strength endured to oversee the work and make important suggestions for his benefit.

Of course, this necessitated numerous visits to the invalid, and it was while returning from one of these that Mr. Heath's horse took fright, causing the accident and putting a stop to the project which lay so near the old lord's heart.

Sir William wrote that the disappointment of both the Duke of Falmouth and Lord Norton was so great that he had himself offered to take his cousin's place and finish the copying of the book, while he remained at Middlewich in attendance upon his injured relative and his family.

Lady Linton was jubilant after receiving this letter, for it was evident that Sir William would be detained at Middlewich for quite a while; meantime she would exert all the cunning of which she was mistress to ruin the woman whom she both feared and hated, and thus plant an insurmountable barrier between Rupert and his beautiful *fiancée*.

With this mad scheme in mind, she ascertained Mrs. Alexander's address, and boldly went one morning to face her enemy in her own domain.

But she was bitterly disappointed to learn that she was not in town. She was away on a little trip, the landlady told her; she might be gone a week longer; she might not return even at the end of that time. "The rooms were paid for in advance for three months, so the woman had not asked when they would return, nor whither they were going, but she had heard the young lady say something about a visit to Edinburgh; possibly they had gone there."

So Lady Linton had to rest on her belligerent oars for a season, though she resolved to be on the alert to act as soon as Mrs. Alexander and her daughter should return.

A couple of weeks later she went one morning to do some shopping for Lillian on Oxford street, and just as she was about to enter a fashionable furnishing store the door opened, a lady came out, and—she stood face to face once more with Mrs. Alexander.

An angry red suffused Lady Linton's face, an ominous flash lighted her cold, gray eyes.

"Ah! so you have returned," she said, sharply, and planting herself directly in the path of her foe.

She was looking very lovely—so lovely, indeed, that her ladyship marveled at her beauty. She wore a black silk dress, simply made, but of richest texture, an elegant mantle of black velvet heavily trimmed with jet, a bonnet of the same material, relieved by three graceful ostrich tips of cream-white; and the dainty affair was bewitchingly becoming; her hands were faultlessly gloved, and a single half-blown Lamargue rose had been drawn into one of the fastenings of her mantle, its pale yellow petals nestling lovingly among the rich folds of velvet. There was the daintiest bloom on her cheeks, her eyes were bright, her whole face animated, and she was a woman to attract admiring attention wherever she went.

Lady Linton congratulated herself that her brother was far from London, for she well knew that it would need but one glance at this beautiful picture to bring him a hopeless captive to her feet once more.

Mrs. Alexander slightly raised her brows at her ladyship's abrupt manner of address, bowed politely, and would have passed on, but the other laid a detaining hand upon her arm, and drew her into a little vestibule just inside the door.

"I want to speak to you," she said, authoritatively.

"Certainly; I am at your service, Lady Linton," was the quiet, lady-like reply, and Virgie's full, blue eyes looked calmly down upon the sallow countenance before her, as she waited to learn why she had been so unceremoniously detained.

"Why have you come to London?" Lady Linton inquired, brusquely.

Mrs. Alexander drew herself up a trifle, and hesitated a moment before replying; then she said, gravely:

"Partly upon business; partly for health."

"Health!" scornfully repeated Lady Linton, with a quick upward glance into that beautiful, blooming face.

A musical laugh rippled over Mrs. Alexander's lips, and she flushed an exquisite color; for both glance and emphasis, although not so intended, were a marked compliment to her appearance.

"You think I do not need to go anywhere in search of health," she observed. "That is true, just now, although I was far from well when I left America."

"What is your 'business' here?" demanded her companion, ignoring her reply.

"Really, Lady Linton," Mrs. Alexander returned, coldly, "I do not know as I feel obliged to explain that to you just yet."

"Just yet!" repeated the other, with a sudden heart-bound. "What am I to understand by that?"

"Just what you choose, Lady Linton."

"Is your 'business' connected in any way with that threat which you made in my presence more than eight years ago?"

"Ah! then you have not forgotten what happened more than eight years ago?"

Lady Linton colored angrily.

"I could almost wish that I had died then, rather than that you should have saved me!" she said, passionately.

"Why?"

Gravely, almost solemnly, the brief inquiry was made.

"Because I hate you! You came between me and some of my brightest hopes. Because you——"

"No, it is not wholly that," Virgie interposed quietly, while her grave, beautiful eyes searched Lady Linton's face, with something of pity in them: "It is because you have injured me, and one is apt to dislike and shrink from another whom one has wronged."

"How have I wronged you?" demanded Lady Linton, in a startled tone, and wondering how much the woman knew.

"I do not need to tell you. Your own conscience needs no other accuser than itself," was the calm reply. "But it would have been far better had your ladyship constituted yourself my friend instead of my enemy."

"I could never be your friend. I shall be your foe to the bitter end, and it was to warn you of this that I detained you to-day. If you have come to London with the intention of thrusting yourself and your daughter upon my brother, let me tell you to beware! You are a divorced woman; you have no claim whatever upon Sir William Heath, and your child shall never be acknowledged by his name. I have vowed this, and I mean it. You may think it all an idle threat, but if you are in London one month from to-day it will be at your peril. I will ruin you. I will so shame and humiliate you that you will be glad to hide yourself from all who know you. I will do even worse if need be. Nothing shall hinder me from making sure work this time."

She was actually hoarse with passion as she concluded.

"This time, Lady Linton? Then it was your work that other time. You acknowledge it?" said Mrs. Alexander, in a calm tone, and without a trace of excitement in either face or manner.

She was as unruffled as when Lady Linton first met her; she had not even lost a vestige of color. All the change that was visible in her was a half-sorrowful light in her beautiful blue eyes, a grave, pitiful expression about her mouth.

Lady Linton saw instantly that she had made a mistake; in her anger and hatred she had admitted more than was wise or prudent, and she grew very pale.

"I acknowledge nothing; I only warn you," she said, almost fiercely.

"Lady Linton," her companion answered composedly, "your threats do not move me; they cannot hurt me, and I fear they will but recoil upon your own head. Believe me, I would much rather be upon friendly terms with you. I feel more like forgiving the injuries of the past than cherishing hostile feelings. I could even at this moment take your hand—the hand that wrote such cruel things of me so many years ago—and say, 'Let us be at peace;' but you will not, and I must go my way and leave you to go yours, hoping that before it is too late for repentance to avail you anything, a better spirit may possess you."

"You defy me then?" said Lady Linton, through tightly closed teeth.

"Oh, no; I do not defy you," was the pleasant rejoinder. "You are very angry, Lady Linton, because I will not allow myself to be frightened and browbeaten by you, but you will feel differently by and by when you come to consider matters in another light. I would rather do you a kindness than harm, and, by the way, I have a package belonging to you which I mean to return to you very soon."

"A package belonging to me! Where did you get it?"

"It is one that I have had many years, but I have only recently discovered that it is yours."

"It is impossible that you can have anything of mine," returned Lady Linton, coldly.

Her companion smiled slightly, then said:

"An uncle of mine was returning from the far East some twelve or thirteen years ago, and, on his way from London to Edinburgh, rode in the same railway carriage with a lady who got out at one of the way stations. He never knew which station it was, for he had fallen asleep shortly after leaving London, and when he awoke she was gone. He found a package, however, which she had dropped and which he could not return, because there was no name upon it, therefore he was forced to take it home to America with him. He confided it to me on his death-bed with the injunction to return it to the owner if I should ever be so fortunate as to meet her. I discovered on the evening of our meeting at Lady Dunforth's that you were the owner."

"I assure you that you are mistaken. I never lost a package in a railway carriage," returned Lady Linton, haughtily.

"No, but a friend to whom you confided it, lost it."

"What—who?" demanded her ladyship, with a start.

"The way I learned that it belonged to you," Mrs. Alexander resumed, "was by observing upon the panel of your carriage door, as I left Lady Dunforth's that evening, the Linton coat of arms. The seal upon the package of which I speak is stamped with a shield bearing a patriarchal cross and the motto 'Droit et Loyal,' and there is also written upon the wrapper this sentence, 'To be destroyed unopened in the event of my death.'"

Lady Linton had shrunk back appalled during this description, and now stood leaning against the wall, white, trembling while great beads of perspiration stood about her mouth and on her forehead.

"Great heavens! have you got that?" at last burst from her quivering lips, in a tone or horror.

"Yes! it is a singular coincidence, is it not?" inquired her companion, serenely. "However, I will return it to you very soon. And now, good-morning, Lady Linton. This will be a very busy day for me, and I must not tarry longer."

With these words, Virginia Alexander swept by the stricken woman with a courteous inclination of her head, and went on her way, apparently unruffled by anything that had occurred during the spirited interview with her sworn enemy, Sir William Heath's sister.

Lady Linton stood for a moment or two utterly motionless, almost paralyzed by the startling revelations which her brother's former wife had just made to her, and then she, too, tottered from the place, murmuring:

"To think that she, of all persons, should have had that during these years! What a fool I have been! But," she continued, with an ominous glitter in her steely eyes, "the die is cast—it will now take desperate measures indeed to secure my own safety and accomplish her defeat."

She returned directly home, for she had neither the strength nor the heart to purchase fashionable gewgaws for Lillian; at least until she had recovered somewhat from the shock she had just received.

Upon her arrival she found still another letter from Sir William awaiting her, and one which filled her with astonishment and put an entirely different aspect upon the future, while a portion, at least, of its contents was calculated to electrify his whole household as well as society at large.

CHAPTER XX.
A STARTLING ANNOUNCEMENT.

Lady Linton's letter was handed to her by the butler just as she was sitting down to lunch.

She had come in just as the bell rang, and leaving her bonnet and wraps in the hall, went directly to the dining-room without going, as usual, to her room to make a change in her toilet; she was far too weary and shaken to mount the stairs.

She broke the seal absently, and began to read in a listless, preoccupied way, when all at once she uttered a startled exclamation, and the paper dropped from her nerveless fingers upon the table.

"Why, mamma, what is it? You are as pale as a ghost. Is Cousin William worse or—dead?" exclaimed Lillian, regarding her mother with mingled curiosity and astonishment.

"No, but the strangest thing in the world has happened."

"It must be something strange to disturb your equanimity like this; but what is it?" inquired the girl, eagerly.

"Your Uncle William is going to be married!"

"You cannot mean it, mamma?—at last!" cried Lillian, amazed; then she added, with a gay laugh: "The dear old bachelor! Well, you will have your wish, after all. You have wanted him to marry for the last dozen years."

"Yes; and—I am glad—I am delighted!" replied Lady Linton, slowly, but with strange exultation in her voice, while her eyes gleamed with almost ferocious triumph.

"Well, I am astonished. I had given Uncle Will up as a hardened case," Lillian said, growing more and more surprised, as she considered the matter; "but do tell me who is the happy woman?"

"A niece of Lord Norton who has just died; you know we read of his death last week, and I have been wondering why your uncle did not write. This accounts for it," replied Lady Linton. Then taking up his letter, she continued: "I will read you what he says. The epistle is very brief, and does not sound like him at all, but I suppose we must excuse it under the circumstances."

"'You will doubtless be surprised by the contents of this letter,' he writes, 'and as I have much on my mind, I will simply state bare facts, leaving details until my return. You already know of my having taken my cousin's place as temporary amanuensis to Lord Norton. I was enabled to complete the manuscript for him the week before his death, which occurred on the ninth. But, during my visits to him, I met a niece of his, who, I may say, is the most beautiful woman I have ever seen. By his lordship's will she becomes the heiress to all his possessions, which consist of his fine estate called Englewood, here in Chester, besides a large amount of personal property. To make a long story short, however, I am going to make this lady my wife, and as I am too old to waste any time upon forms or so-called etiquette, we intend to be married immediately—that is, within the month—about the twenty-first, I think, after which we shall repair to Heathdale, where we shall quietly remain for the present. The wedding will be strictly private on account of his lordship's recent death and in compliance with the request of his niece. I will, however, notify you further of my plans before the twenty-first.'"

The epistle closed abruptly and rather formally, and Lady Linton's face was crimson as she concluded the reading of it.

"It is the most unheard of thing in the world!" she said, excitedly. "A private wedding, indeed—not even his own sister invited, and it is all so sudden that it fairly takes my breath away."

"They might at least have asked us to go to Englewood to witness the ceremony," Lillian observed, thoughtfully. "The letter doesn't sound a bit like Uncle Will."

"I suppose he is so taken up with his bride-elect that he has not much time or thought for any one else; but he might have told us something about her; he did not even mention her name; I suppose, however, we are to infer that she is a Miss Norton. I wonder whether she is young or old?" Lady Linton said, in an injured tone, and looking both perplexed and annoyed.

"He says she is beautiful, mamma."

"Of course; one's betrothed is always beautiful to the man who is to be married. They are going directly to Heathdale," she added, musingly. "There ought to be some one there to receive them, and the house needs preparation for the occasion. I think, Lillian, that, notwithstanding I have been rather shabbily treated in this affair, I shall go down to Heathdale and give them the best welcome possible at so short a notice. I can at least brighten things up and arrange for a small dinner-party and reception in honor of the bride."

"Perhaps they would prefer not to meet anyone just yet, mamma," Lillian suggested.

"I cannot help it. Such a home-coming as that would be too dismal, and not at all in keeping with the dignity of the family. I shall take matters into my own hands and conduct the affair as I think best. We will go to Heathdale the last of the week."

Her ladyship fell into a profound reverie after announcing this decision, while Lillian took up the morning paper and began to read.

Lady Linton was deeply hurt by the way that her brother had written of his approaching marriage, and more so at having been ignored in all the arrangements; yet in spite of all this she was secretly jubilant over the fact that Sir William was about to bring a mistress to Heathdale. It would relieve her of a great burden; of all further plotting and intrigue regarding the enemy whom she had encountered only that day. Virginia Alexander might do her worst now—once let the twenty-first of December pass and she need fear her no more. She might succeed in securing an acknowledgment from Sir William that Virgie was his lawful child and a settlement of a portion of his property upon her; but there would be no longer any fear of the long-parted husband and wife coming to an understanding with each other—she, at least, would never come to Heathdale to queen it as mistress.

She had heard of Lord Norton. He was reputed to be very old, very eccentric, and very literary; but she had not known of what his family consisted. She did not know, even now, farther than that he had a niece, but in her present mood, with that bitter hatred against Virginia Alexander rankling in her heart and the fear that her own past treachery was liable to be exposed if she was ever allowed to enter Heathdale, she was prepared to welcome Lord Norton's heiress in the most cordial manner, and her spirits rose light as air at the prospect of a new sister-in-law.

"Mamma," said Lillian, suddenly looking up from her paper and breaking in upon these musings, "Uncle Will's engagement is announced here."

"What! in the paper? Well, I must say they are rushing things."

She held out her hand for the sheet, an evil smile on her thin lips, as she imagined something of the chagrin and disappointment that Mrs. Alexander would experience upon reading an account of Sir William Heath's approaching marriage.

There was quite an extended paragraph regarding it, considerable being said about the late Lord Norton and his recent death; mention being made of his having left the whole of his large property to a niece; while the fact that Sir William Heath was contemplating matrimony with the "beautiful heiress," gave rise to some pleasantry, since the "distinguished baronet having for so many years resisted Cupid's most artful endeavors to lead him to Hymen's altar, his friends and well-wishers had begun to fear that he was hopelessly invulnerable."

"Mamma, what will become of us when Uncle Will brings his wife home?" Lillian asked, somewhat anxiously, as Lady Linton laid down the paper.

The same question had been agitating her ladyship's mind.

They could not well go to Linton Grange, for Percy was making extensive improvements in view of his own approaching marriage; they had no home of their own—in fact they were wholly dependent upon Sir William, and Lady Linton felt that no place but Heathdale would ever be like home to her.

"We will not borrow trouble about that, Lillian," she answered, "this Miss Norton may be very young and inexperienced; in that case she would need some older person, like myself, to advise and assist her; so I imagine that we shall still be welcome in your uncle's household."

That evening, at a dinner-party, Lady Linton was besieged by numerous friends with questions regarding her brother's engagement.

She looked wise, and appeared as if she had been in the secret for some time but had not been allowed to divulge anything.

It was true, she admitted, that the marriage was rather a sudden one; but of course it could not have occurred before, because of Lord Norton's critical condition, and there was no reason now why it should not take place, except for etiquette's sake, and her brother did not propose to defer their happiness simply to observe a law of fashion. They would not, however, appear in society at present, she affirmed, but remain quietly at Heathdale, perhaps until another season, while there would only be an informal reception of their oldest friends, at their home-coming, and to arrange for this she was herself going to Heathdale.

She appeared to be very much elated over the marriage, spoke eloquently of the bride-elect, of her grace, beauty, and intelligence; for she was far too proud to allow it to be known that she had been taken as much by surprise as society at large by the announcement of the event.

To Mrs. Farnum alone she acknowledged it; for that lady called the next day, and had asked her point-blank some questions which she could not answer, and she had been obliged to confess that she "did not know."

"Well, Miriam," said her friend, "it is rather hard on you, I own, not to be consulted, or even asked to the wedding, but your heart will be set at rest on one subject—you need not fear that Alexander woman any more after the twenty-first."

"No; she may do her worst then. I have lived in daily terror lest she should meet William and everything would be explained. What do you think, Myra?" asked Lady Linton, suddenly. "She has got that diary!"

"What diary?"

"That one I gave to you to keep for me, the summer I was on the Continent—the diary you lost!"

"Miriam Linton! how came she by it?" cried Mrs. Farnum, aghast.

"She says her uncle was in the railway carriage with you when you left London that afternoon after I had met you at the —— Hotel, and you dropped it in the coach."

"Well, I am at least glad to know *how* I lost it," returned her friend, in a relieved tone. "It has been a most annoying mystery to me all these years. Does she know what there is in it?"

"I do not know," Lady Linton said, growing pale. "I met her yesterday on Oxford street, when she told me she had it, and would return it soon. If she has not opened the package, I am all right; if she has, and ever sees fit to betray me to Sir William, it will be a sad day for me."

"You were very foolish ever to commit to paper anything concerning that American escapade."

"I suppose I was, but I always keep a diary; there are many things of importance that I like to remember accurately, and a diary is so convenient to refer to—it has saved me many mistakes."

"It would have been far better if you had destroyed *that* year's notes, as I advised you," returned Mrs. Farnum.

"But it was full of important data, and I never dreamed that anything could happen to it—it was very careless of you to lose it," said her ladyship, complainingly.

"I know it was, and I have suffered a great deal of anxiety on account of it; for, of course, with all those names and dates, I am implicated almost as much as yourself. Why don't you go around to her lodgings and get it at once?—your mind will be at rest then. If the seal has never been broken, you are as safe as if it had never been lost."

"True; I believe I will," Lady Linton answered, brightening.

She followed the advice of her friend the very next day, and, calling at Mrs. Alexander's lodgings, was shown at once up to her private parlor.

There was no one there when she entered, but presently Virgie came in, looking charming in her morning robe of mauve cashmere, with blue silk facings, and greeted her ladyship politely, although with some reserve.

"You wished to see mamma," she said, "but I am obliged to receive you as she is not in just now. Can I do anything for you, Lady Linton?"

"I wished to see Mrs. Alexander personally," returned Lady Linton, haughtily. "Will she return soon?"

"I am afraid not. She had an engagement with Madame Gerbier, her modiste, at eleven, and one with her lawyer at one," Virgie explained.

Lady Linton thought a moment, then she said:

"Mrs. Alexander told me, a day or two ago, that she had a package belonging to me; do you know anything about it?"

"A package?" repeated Virgie, looking mystified; then she added, quickly, "Oh! perhaps it is that sealed package that mamma's uncle found so long ago. Is that yours, Lady Linton?"

"Yes. Sealed!—did you say it is *sealed?*" asked the woman, breathlessly.

"Yes, it is sealed with a strange device and motto."

"And has it never been opened?" was the eager query.

"Of course not; it is just as mamma's uncle found it," Virgie responded, with curling lips, and flushing indignantly at the implied suspicion of the woman.

Lady Linton could have wept for joy. She was saved! her vile secrets were still all her own; and if she could but get that coveted diary into her possession once again, she had nothing to fear; she would burn it without a moment's hesitation.

"I am very sorry to miss Mrs. Alexander; but perhaps *you* could get it for me?" she said, insinuatingly.

"I do not think I should like to do that without mamma's sanction," Virgie answered; "but I will tell her your errand, and no doubt she will take measures to return the package to you at once."

"Very well," replied Lady Linton; "tell her to send it immediately to my brother's residence; the street and number are on my card, which you have. I shall leave town to-morrow, and would like it before I go."

Virgie promised to deliver the message, and her ladyship took her leave, with a heart lighter than she had known for years, for the burden of a great dread had been rolled from it.

But she did not receive the package before leaving for Heathdale, as she had confidently expected.

She had arranged to go on the fifteenth, taking Lillian with her, and although she waited until the last minute, hoping for the appearance of her long-lost diary, she was obliged to depart without it.

She did not worry over it very much, however, for she told herself that if it had been kept all these years with the seal unbroken, there was not much danger of its being disturbed at this late day.

Just as she was about to enter the carriage there arrived a telegram from her brother. It contained just two lines:

"Shall leave Englewood Wednesday noon; arrive at Heathdale on the 7:30 express. Meet us there if you like."

"Rather a curt bidding to a wedding feast," Lady Linton sarcastically observed, showing it to her daughter; but she would have been more than content had she not been bidden at all, for her brother's marriage was, to her, an unlooked-for triumph over her enemy, a release from a much dreaded doom.

CHAPTER XXI.
THE ARRIVAL AT HEATHDALE.

Upon her arrival at Heathdale, Lady Linton was considerably surprised to find that Sir William had engaged the services of a professional decorator to prepare his home for the reception of his bride, and great improvements had been made in many of the rooms. The suite over the library, and looking out upon the river, had been exquisitely fitted up in blue and white, and gold for his wife's special use, while several new pictures and pieces of statuary had been added to the already choice collection which the old mansion possessed.

Still, with all this added elegance, it needed the touch of a tasteful woman's hand to make it really home-like, and both Lady Linton and her daughter exerted themselves to make everything as attractive as possible.

Her ladyship realized that perhaps she was presuming a little beyond her jurisdiction in arranging, unauthorized, for a dinner-party, but she was determined to do honor to the new mistress of Heathdale, and to show her brother her entire approval of the step he had taken. She was bound, too, that no funereal gloom should hang over their first evening at home, but that all things should wear a joyous and inviting aspect; so she sent invitations to a select few to come and welcome the baronet and his bride upon their arrival.

The eventful day at length dawned—a bright, beautiful winter's day, yet mild for the season, and, at an early hour, the household at Heathdale was all astir, and preparations for the grand event went briskly forward; for everyone, down to the lowest servant, loved the master, and was eager to show him honor on this unlooked-for occasion, while all were on the alert to learn what manner of a wife he was about to bring home.

The state dining-room was handsomely decorated for the grand event; the best plate had been polished to the last degree of brightness, the finest linen bleached and pressed, and a most sumptuous dinner was in preparation.

There were flowers, choice and rare, everywhere, and every room was fragrant with their perfume and bright with their beauty.

A glowing fire was built in the great hall, while over the carved mantle above the huge fire-place, Lady Linton had caused to be placed a beautiful shield, representing the crest of her family, and composed of lilies and roses, with the word "Welcome," in immortelles, surmounting it.

At seven o'clock the guests began to gather; there were the Hon. Mr. Capron with his wife and daughter, from an adjoining estate. The rector and his genial helpmate; Lord Alfred Hartington, and his sister; Percy Linton and his charming *fiancée*; Mrs. Farnum with Lord and Lady Royalston. Rupert had of course been included in the list, but, not having yet arrived, was looked for on the train from London, that was due a few minutes before the one from the west.

Lady Linton was magnificent in garnet velvet, point lace, and diamonds. She had spared neither time nor money for the occasion, and really had never looked so well as now.

Lillian wore simple white silk, with crimson roses, in which she was brilliantly handsome.

The remainder of the party were equally well arrayed, and it was truly a goodly company that gathered to welcome the Baron of Heathdale.

At precisely a quarter to eight a carriage was heard to arrive, and Lady Linton hastened to the hall to be the first to welcome her brother and his wife; but she started back, almost affrighted, as she beheld instead, William Heath, looking pale and thin, but bright and smiling, enter, leaning upon Rupert Hamilton's arm, and followed by his wife and son.

"Where is my brother?" she inquired, after greeting them all most cordially.

Rupert smiled roguishly as he replied:

"They have achieved a flank movement upon you, Lady Linton; when they saw the house ablaze, they suspected a reception, and as a bride would naturally be somewhat sensitive about appearing before company in travel-stained garments, Sir William and Lady Heath drove to the side-entrance, and doubtless are now in their own rooms. I am commissioned to make their excuses, and to beg that you will send word when dinner will be served."

Lady Linton at once dispatched a servant to tell his master that dinner had been ordered at nine o'clock, but it could be delayed if he desired.

Sir William returned answer not to make any change, that he and Lady Heath would be ready to meet their friends by half-past eight.

The time would have passed heavily after that, had it not been for Rupert, who was a general favorite, and soon had the whole company in the best possible humor with themselves and everybody else, and Lady Linton blessed him in her heart for his genial mirth, his exhaustless fund of anecdote and repartee.

She was very restless, however, and anxiously watched the clock upon the mantle, while it seemed as if half-past eight would never arrive.

All at once she saw Rupert dart from the side of Lillian, with whom he had been talking, toward the lower door of the drawing-room, and disappear in the hall.

Then there came a murmur of surprise from the opposite direction, and glancing toward the upper door, she saw Sir William standing there, smiling and looking the personification of joy, with a beautiful woman leaning upon his arm.

Lady Linton started eagerly forward to greet them, when, all at once, her heart bounded into her throat with suffocating force, a blur came before her eyes, her limbs trembled and almost sank beneath her.

What delusion was this—what trick of her fancy?

Was it a horrible nightmare, or had some sorceress suddenly bewitched her sight.

She covered her eyes with her hand for a moment, and then looked again.

No, it was no delusion—it was no trick; for just before her, looking like a queen in her rich robes, her face radiant with happiness as she leaned proudly upon her husband's arm, she saw the woman who she had hated and wronged for long, long years; whom she had plotted to ruin and sweep from her path forever—Virginia Alexander! the chosen bride of her brother in his youth, and now, in spite of falsehood, calumny, treachery and even divorce, his happy wife, and the mistress of Heathdale!

She was clad in a reception robe of pale lavender velvet, simply piped with satin; it faultlessly fitted her perfect form, while its ample train, sweeping out behind her, made her stately figure seem more regal than usual. Diamonds of purest water sparkled in her ears, gleamed upon her bosom, and an exquisite crescent was fastened among the glossy coils of her still rich and abundant hair.

Never had she been more beautiful, even in her youth, than now, as she stood upon the threshold of her new home, where she was destined to reign for long years yet, an honored and idolized wife.

Happiness had done much for her during the last few weeks; her face had resumed its rounded outlines; a delicate bloom had come into her cheeks; her lips were like lines of brightest coral; her eyes brilliant with the exhilaration caused by the restoration of blissful hopes.

Just behind her, and now attended by Rupert Hamilton, was Virgie, inexpressibly lovely in cream-white silk, with no ornaments save a bunch of fragrant mignonette in her corsage; but, in the eyes of her lover, and to others gathered there, she seemed the fairest vision of youth that they had ever looked upon.

Lady Linton afterward confessed that she suffered more than death in the brief interval that elapsed before her brother led his bride cross the threshold and advanced to greet her.

But she was a woman of indomitable will, and, though her spirit for a moment recoiled beneath this unexpected blow, she resolutely rallied her failing courage—an almost uncontrollable rage took possession of her as she realized how she had been duped—fooled; how this overwhelming surprise had been deliberately prepared for her, and, though she was as colorless as the costly lace that was fluttering upon her bosom with every pulsation of her fiercely bounding heart, she swept haughtily toward that regal-looking couple until within a few feet of them, when she made a profound obeisance before them, saying with formal politeness:

"Welcome, Sir William and Lady Heath, to Heathdale."

She met and bore her defeat superbly, although she was sick at heart and almost in a frenzy of anger, mortification, and humiliation, at being thus triumphantly confronted in her own home by the woman, whom, all her life, she had schemed to crush. To think that she should have made all these elaborate preparations and planned this brilliant welcome but to suffer such an ignominious overthrow in Virginia Alexander's very presence, was maddening beyond description.

But she would rather have died than betray anything of the conflict within her, and, after that one obeisance, she stepped aside to allow others to offer their greetings and congratulations, and by the time supper was announced she had recovered, to all outward appearances at least, entire control of herself.

Sir William led the way to the dining-room, and, without one word to his sister, conducted his wife to the head of the table, whispering fondly as he seated her:

"Welcome, my darling, to your home and to your position as mistress of Heathdale."

He then sought his own place opposite, while the butler seated the other guests according to their rank.

There were two others among that company who had recognized the new mistress of Heathdale with fear and trembling—Mrs. Farnum and her daughter, Lady Royalston.

But, judging from Lady Heath's gracious manner and the attention which she bestowed upon all her guests alike, there was not one among the company whom she did not regard in the most friendly way.

She was simply charming; her bearing and all her observances of etiquette were faultless, and once, during the meal, Lady Royalston bent and whispered in her mother's ear:

"This is the woman whom Lady Linton scorned as unfit to mate with a Heath! This is the woman whom we lent our aid to ruin! Mamma, we ought to go down on our knees to her and her lovely daughter whom we have so wronged."

"For Heaven's sake, Sadie, do not add to my torture," returned Mrs. Farnum, with pale lips. "Remember it was all for you—I knew that you loved——"

"That will do, mamma; we will never open that grave again," returned Lady Royalston, losing some of her own color, "but I would give much to be able to have Lady Heath for my friend, and I am impressed that we shall never be bidden to Heathdale again."

After dinner, an hour or more was spent in social intercourse, during which something of Sir William's and Lady Heath's story was divulged.

The baronet had insisted upon this, for Virgie's sake.

"She is my own daughter, and I must claim her as such before the whole world," he said, so as much as he deemed advisable to relate, without publicly compromising any one who had been instrumental in causing the misunderstanding between himself and his wife, he told to his friends.

It was also announced at the same time that Mr. Hamilton, the baronet's ward, had won the baronet's beautiful daughter, and that there would be another wedding about Easter.

When Lady Linton heard this she looked around for Lillian, but she had quietly withdrawn from the company directly after dinner, and did not make her appearance again.

The evening was over at last, and the guests dispersed, pronouncing Lady Heath "delightful," and predicting a happy future for the master of Heathdale after the romantic trials of his youth and the sorrow of his later years.

When Mrs. Farnum and her daughter took leave of Sir William and his bride, the baronet simply bowed to them without offering his hand, saying, with the least possible but unmistakable emphasis:

"Good-by, Mrs. Farnum; adieu, Lady Royalston." And both knew that all the past had been explained, and they had received their final *congé*.

Lady Royalston's prediction had been verified.

When the last guest had departed, Sir William turned to his sister, his face stern and cold.

"Miriam," he said, in a tone that made her shiver, "at last I have found my Virgie, my mountain maid whom I have loved all my life long. But what of the lost years of the past?—the sorrow, the loneliness, and misunderstanding? What of the hatred and treachery that produced it all?"

Every word fell upon Lady Linton's heart as if it had been a blow from a hammer.

She made a gesture of despair. She could not speak; she felt that she should go mad unless she could soon get away to the quiet of her room and be released from that fearful constraint which she had imposed upon herself for so many hours.

Lady Heath read something of her suffering in that wild gesture, and she laid her lips against her husband's ear, whispering:

"Dear Will, we can afford to be generous out of the abundance of our happiness."

Sir William's face melted into infinite tenderness at her plea.

He placed his arm about her waist and drew her fondly to him.

"If you can plead for her, my darling, I should not be obdurate," he murmured, tenderly; then, turning again to his sister, he added: "We will talk further of this matter to-morrow. Good-night, Miriam."

With one more stern glance at the unhappy woman, he led his beautiful wife from the room, and Lady Linton, her strength exhausted, her proud spirit crushed, sank with a moan of anguish to the floor, and there the butler found her half an hour later when he came to put out the lights.

He called her maid, and together they helped her to her room, where she spent half the night in hysterics, and then, worn out, sank into a profound slumber or stupor.

CHAPTER XXII.
A BACKWARD GLANCE.

In order to more fully comprehend the events related in the last chapter we must go back to the day following Lady Dunforth's reception, when Mrs. Alexander's lawyer, Mr. Thurston, called and held a protracted interview with her.

She had consulted him soon after arriving in London, and, after gathering all the information possible regarding her history, he informed her that there would be no difficulty whatever in establishing Virgie's claim, as a daughter of the House of Heath, and this morning he had called to tell her that he was ready to arrange a meeting with Sir William whenever she felt equal to the trial.

"Must I meet him!" she asked, growing faint at the thought.

"It will be best for both you and Miss Alexander to meet him at the outset, for, of course, if he is at all inclined to contest the claim, he will at once demand the proof of your identity," Mr. Thurston replied.

Mrs. Alexander felt that this would be a severer test upon her strength than she had anticipated.

She did not wish to meet Sir William, and yet at the same time there was an almost uncontrollable longing in her heart to see him once more. If she could look upon him without his seeing her, it would be all she would ask; she shrank from forcing herself upon his presence.

Still if it must be, she resolved to brace herself for the interview; she had determined that he should acknowledge Virgie as his child, and nothing should deter her from accomplishing her object.

"Very well," she said, "I will be governed wholly by your advice. But what is this?" she added, as he laid a paper before her.

"I simply desire your signature to this document as a mere matter of form," the lawyer told her.

Mrs. Alexander signed it and passed it back to him.

"Virginia N. Alexander," he read; then he started.

"What is your middle name?" he asked.

"Norton. My grandmother was an English woman, by that name, before her marriage."

"What was her Christian name?" Mr. Thurston asked, eagerly.

"Nora."

"Whom did she marry?"

"A man by the name of Charles Bradford. They went to America soon after their marriage and settled in California," Mrs. Alexander replied, wondering why the lawyer should question her thus regarding her family.

"Did your grandmother have any brothers or sisters?"

"I believe there was a brother—Albert by name—for I have heard my mother, who was called Alberta, say that she was named for an uncle; but I never knew anything of him, as he lived in England, and, after my grandmother's death, all communication between the families ceased. It was a whim of hers to call me Virginia Norton, for she said she did not wish the family name to die out entirely."

Mr. Thurston changed color and began to look excited. He drew a set of tablets from his pocket, and, opening them, examined several entries therein.

"Mrs. Alexander," he said at last, "I believe you have at last unwittingly solved a riddle that has been a very complicated one to me and my partner for the last two years, and which we had almost despaired of ever solving."

"How can that be?" she asked, greatly surprised.

"Listen, and I will tell you," said the lawyer. "There is living in Cheshire County, England, a man by the name of Lord Albert Norton——"

"Oh, I do not think there was ever any title in our family," Mrs. Alexander interrupted, smiling. "I am sure they were people in moderate circumstances, as my grandfather went to America to try to improve his condition in life."

"Lord Albert Norton was a comparatively poor man himself until he was over fifty years of age," Mr. Thurston went on, composedly, "when he published some literary works of great merit. He began about that time to interest himself in political affairs, and was created a peer of the realm in 1840. He has been a very eccentric man, has never married, but devoted himself almost wholly to literature and politics. He has amassed wealth rapidly during the later years of his life, for, having no one but himself on whom to expend it, his income has accumulated. He seldom went into society and rarely entertained in his own home. He is now about ninety years of age, and although very feeble in body, his mind appears to be as vigorous as ever.

"Two years ago he applied to us to look up some relatives who went to America many years ago. We were authorized to make thorough work and spare no expense, for his lordship was anxious that his property should go to some of his kindred rather than to the crown after his death. We traced

Nora Norton Bradford to California, but she had been dead many years. We found she had had a daughter Alberta who had married a man by the name of Alexander. She and her husband were also dead; their graves were found in the Lone Mountain cemetery, San Francisco. We learned that they, too, had a daughter by the name of Virginia, but she had disappeared from the city several years ago, and no trace of her could be found; not until I saw your signature this morning did it occur to me that I had found the heir for whom Lord Norton commissioned us to search so long ago."

Mrs. Alexander looked up with a pale, wondering face.

"Do you mean to imply that I am Lord Norton's heir?" she asked, in an agitated tone.

"Exactly," replied Mr. Thurston, confidently, "judging from what you have told me there can be no doubt of it. I suppose that you have proofs of your identity, however?"

"Yes, I have my marriage certificate and an old Bible that belonged to my grandmother, which contains, in her own handwriting, the date of her birth and marriage, also that of her husband's death and my mother's birth."

"That will be ample proof. And now, Mrs. Alexander, as Lord Norton is in a very critical condition, being liable to drop away any day, we must go to Chester immediately. When can you be ready?"

"In an hour, if necessary," she replied, "but it does not seem possible that I can be related to this gentleman! I cannot realize it—a peer of the realm!" she quoted to herself with a strange smile.

"We will submit our evidence to his lordship himself and see what his verdict will be," returned Mr. Thurston, smiling. "A train will leave for Liverpool at two this afternoon. Chester is a few miles this side, and we will avail ourselves of that, if agreeable to you."

"Very well; I submit myself wholly to your guidance, in this matter," Mrs. Alexander responded. "Meantime, I suppose, my other business will have to wait."

"I should advise it; as Lord Norton is in such a critical condition, every moment is precious. It will be far better for him to recognize you as his heir, than to be obliged to prove it after his death; and, madam, you will occupy no mean position if you become the mistress of Englewood, which is the name of his fine estate."

Mr. Thurston then took his leave, promising to call in season to accompany her to the train, and then the still wondering woman sought Virgie and related the marvelous tale to her.

This was the business that called them so suddenly from London, and which was destined to bring about even greater changes in their lives before their return.

They arrived at Englewood late in the evening, and found his lordship's carriage awaiting them at the station, for Mr. Thurston had telegraphed of his coming, and stated that he should bring two ladies with him.

They found Englewood, at least what they were able to see of it, a delightful place. The house, a massive structure of stone, was an ancient affair, but it had been well preserved, and although it was the home of an eccentric old bachelor, was a most comfortable and home-like dwelling. Evidently his lordship knew and appreciated the luxuries of life.

The following morning, Mr. Thurston had an interview with the invalid and informed him of his recent discovery.

Lord Norton expressed himself very much delighted with the news, and appeared very eager to make the acquaintance of his grand-niece and her daughter.

Accordingly, after he was somewhat rested, Mr. Thurston conducted the ladies into his presence, and the moment his eye rested upon Mrs. Alexander, he declared his conviction that she was a Norton; "her features are very like his sister Nora's," he said, "although her grandmother was not nearly as handsome," he added, with a twinkle of humor about his mouth.

The old Bible and marriage certificate were brought to him, and confirmed his statement regarding the relationship. He recognized his sister's handwriting immediately, and produced some of her letters to compare with it.

"There can be no doubt," Mr. Thurston said, after a careful examination of the chirography, "and I congratulate you, my lord, upon the fulfillment of your desire; and you, madam," turning to his client, "upon having discovered your relative."

"Will you stay with me, Virginia?" the old man asked, turning a wistful glance upon the beautiful woman. "It will not be for long," he added; "the sands of my life are nearly run out; a few days, or weeks at the most, will end my life, and it will be pleasant to feel that some of my own kin are near me at the last."

Yes, his niece said, she would stay; her heart went out with a feeling of pity and tenderness toward the man, who all his life, had lived in such loneliness and isolation, and she resolved that she would devote herself exclusively to his comfort during the little while that he remained upon earth.

Mr. Thurston was detained a day or two to attend to some business, relating to the will, which gave everything, with the exception of some annuities to old servants, to Virginia Alexander and her heirs forever.

She had come to Englewood on the very day of Mr. William Heath's accident, and it was the following morning, at the very hour of her first interview with her uncle, that Sir William Heath received the telegram announcing his cousin's critical condition.

He, too, left on the two o'clock train for Liverpool, reaching Middlewich about the same time that Mrs. Alexander had arrived at Englewood the night before.

It was three days later, that in accordance with his proposition to the Duke of Falmouth to act as amanuensis to Lord Norton in his cousin's place, he went to Englewood to begin his work under the old lord's direction, little dreaming of the surprise and joy in store for him there.

When the butler answered his ring, he stated his business, and was shown directly to the invalid's chamber, where he found him propped up in bed with manuscripts lying all about him, and impatiently awaiting his appearance.

He spent several hours, learning the plan of the work, making notes, and even venturing a few suggestions upon some points regarding which he was well posted, and then took his leave promising to get regularly to work the next day.

As he was following the servant down stairs, the man remarked that his carriage was not ready, but if he would step into the library for a few moments, he would inform him when it came to the door.

He signified his willingness to do so and passed down the wide old hall, which was paneled in oak exquisitively carved, to a lofty room, furnished and frescoed in rich tints, and lined from floor to ceiling with books of every description.

It was a most luxurious apartment, and plainly indicated that the old lord, eccentric though he might be on some points, had loved the elegancies of life. If he had been something of a miser, as report accredited him, it could not have been in anything relating to his own comfort or tastes.

Sir William sat down by a table that was drawn close to a cheerful fire, and, leaning back lazily in the huge lounging chair stationed there, he took up the morning paper which lay open at his hand.

He had read scarcely a dozen lines, when the door behind him opened and some one came forward, saying, in an eager tone:

"Oh, Virgie, I have just found an old Bible up stairs, in which there are records of all family births, marriages, and deaths for many generations; my grandmother's and my mother's are among them and correspond exactly with those I have—ah! excuse me; sir—I thought—oh, Heaven!"——

CHAPTER XXIII.
REUNITED.

Virginia Alexander had gone up to her room less than half an hour previous, leaving Virgie in the library reading, and snugly ensconced in that great lounging chair by the fire.

While looking for something in a closet, she had come across the old Bible referred to, and opening it for examination, she had found a complete genealogical record covering more than a century and a half.

Delighted with her discovery, she hastened back to Virgie—who meantime had stolen out for a little exercise—eager to tell her news, and, coming into the room turning the leaves of the book, she had not noticed that a stranger was there until Sir William suddenly arose, his heart bounding within him at the sound of that well-remembered voice, and turned toward her.

She had not seen him for more than eighteen years, and he had changed far more than she during that time.

Sorrow had saddened him somewhat; he had grown grave and dignified, and his hair had just begun to be streaked with silver. There were lines about his mouth telling of a grief that he had never outgrown, there was a wistful look in his eyes showing that his heart still yearned for the love of his youth. His form, too, had developed; he was broader-shouldered and stouter.

But he was a grand and kingly looking man, and she knew him in a moment.

The color left her face; something seemed to smite her heart with a heavy blow, almost benumbing her, and she put out her hand, catching at the table for support, while the Bible fell heavily to the floor.

But she was very lovely even in her pallor and consternation. She wore a tea-gown of silver-gray, with a dainty fichu of lace and blue ribbons, while, as she arose from the dinner-table an hour before, Virgie had selected some pink and white roses and playfully tucked them in her corsage.

Even during that first blissful year of their wedded life she had never seemed more beautiful or more dear to Sir William Heath than at that moment.

"Virgie," he cried, springing toward her, and would have caught her wildly to his breast, the past all forgotten, conscious only that he had found her, his own loved one, once more!

But she rallied instantly, though she trembled violently and still clung to the table for support.

She put out her hand to stop him.

"Sir William Heath!" she said, weakly, but with a haughty bearing which became her well, and warned him that he must not approach her, causing him to remember, too, that she was his wife no longer, for that dread decree of the divorce court stood between them.

Yet he loved her madly still; his heart recognized her as his wife in spite of all.

"Oh, Virgie, I have found you at last!" he cried, his voice breaking in a great sob.

"At last we meet," she said, with pale lips, although she thrilled at his words, "but I did not think it would be like this. Did you come here to seek me?"

"No, I came upon business with Lord Norton. I never dreamed of finding you here. Where have you been all these long—these endless years? Where is our child? Oh, Virgieseamstresses how can you stand there like that, so cold, so relentless, when you think of that bond between us?"

"But—there is between us a barrier as relentless, as impassable as death!" she murmured, with quivering lips, while a film seemed gathering over her eyes, and her strength almost failed her.

Something in her tone and manner told Sir William, that she still loved him in spite of the misunderstanding of the past, and her present coldness, and his heart leaped with a sweet, new hope.

"Virgie, there is no barrier—there has never been any barrier save that which you yourself have interposed between us," he said, eagerly, and venturing a step nearer to her.

Again she put out her hand to check him—that small, beautiful hand whose rosy finger-tips he had so loved to kiss in those old days.

"Your wife! your son!" she murmured, brokenly.

"I have no wife, Heaven help me!" he cried, the veins standing out full and hard upon his forehead. "What can you mean? I have no son."

"Are they—dead?" she asked, lifting her eyes to his face for the first time since he had first confronted her.

"No," he returned, briefly, trying to comprehend her meaning, for of course he never knew that she had seen his cousin's boy and believed him his.

"No?" Virgie questioned, catching her breath quickly. Was it possible that the beautiful woman he had married had, after long years, discovered his treachery and forsaken him?

"Virgie, my beloved, I never had but one wife," said Sir William, gravely.

She seemed turning to stone at those words.

Had there been some terrible mistake after all? Had she lost eighteen years of happiness when she might have been his loved and loving wife?

"I know," he went on, eagerly, "all about that wretched blunder in the newspapers, when my cousin, William Heath, was mistaken for me. He was married to Miss Margaret Stanhope soon after my return to England, but the notice in the papers read as if I had been married instead. They have a son. Oh, Virgie! is it possible that you have believed Willie was my boy?" he asked, light beginning to break in upon his mind.

A moan of pain broke from the pale woman before him.

"But they told me, Lady Linton wrote; ah! those cruel letters," she faltered, in a voice of anguish.

"Who told you? what has my sister——" Sir William began, but that brave, long suffering heart, could bear no more as it realized all too late, that the bitter past need not have been, and she sank unconscious at his feet before he could complete his sentence.

Sir William sprang forward with a cry of fear, and raised her tenderly in his arms.

He laid her bright head upon his breast; he bent and kissed the fair, pale face with passionate, trembling lips, and held her to his throbbing heart with a clasp that claimed her all his own, in spite of the cruel decree that had parted them for so many years.

But Virgie did not lose herself for more than a moment; the fall partially restored her, and she began to realize what was passing even though she had not strength to assert herself. She knew that she was lying upon the bosom of the man whom she had always loved, and it seemed like a blessed repose to rest there, and to feel his sheltering arms around her after the cares and struggles of the past.

She knew now that he had always loved her, and had been true to her, and that the woman, who for more than eighteen years had been the object of her jealousy and envy was, as far as he was concerned, but a myth—a phantom.

Oh! the delight of knowing that his affection had never wavered, of realizing that he had been as faithful to her as she to him.

Her eyes unclosed and she looked up into the fond face bending over her, and a quick flush of happiness swept up to her brow, as she met the fervent lovelight in his glance.

She sat up and gently released herself from his clinging arms, and he raised and led her to the great chair in which he had been sitting when she entered the room.

At that moment there came a knock on the door and the servant announced that Sir William's carriage was ready.

Sir William controlled his emotion as well as he was able, and turning to the man, said:

"I find I cannot leave for another hour yet, please send the carriage back to the stable, and I will ring when I wish it again."

The man bowed and withdrew, and Sir William turned again to his dear one.

"Are you better, Virgie! Shall I call a maid to get you something?" he asked, regarding her still pale face anxiously.

"No, do not," she pleaded, putting out her hand beseechingly.

"At least let me get you some water," he said, and going to a table where there were an ice pitcher and goblets, he filled a glass, and brought it to her.

She drank thirstily and passed the goblet back to him, looking up with a grateful little smile for the service.

He bent impulsively and touched his lips to her forehead.

"My darling!" he breathed.

Again the quick color flooded her face and tears sprang into her eyes; how she had longed for years to hear those tender tones!

The sight of her tears moved him deeply.

He put down the glass, and kneeling beside her drew her again into his arms.

"Oh, my love!" he whispered, a great sob heaving his broad chest, "you have been cruelly deceived, but set me at rest upon one point—tell me that you love me yet. I have never been untrue to you in thought or deed. I have lived a lonely, solitary life. I have been heart-broken without you. Virgie, you were the one love of my whole life; now tell me if your heart is still mine."

She bowed her head upon his breast, melted by his fond words, and sobbed in an agony of grief for her lost happiness; she twined her arms about his neck and drew his face down to her tear-wet cheek.

"Oh, Will," she murmured, brokenly, "I have ruined all your life and mine! I should have come to you, in spite of all, and to learn my fate from your own lips. We have lost all these years when we might have been so happy. You know that I love you; every day, every hour of my life my heart has cried out for you. I have literally been starving for your love."

He needed no stronger proof of her devotion; he knew that she loved him as fondly now as in those months of their early wedded life, and he folded her still closer to him, kissing, again and again, those dear lips, which for eighteen years had known no caress save what she had received from her child.

Their reunion was perfect and complete, and, for a little while, they could think of nothing, speak of nothing save the joy of being once more all in all to each other.

But at length Sir William insisted that she should tell him all the story of the past; how the first suspicion of his treachery had taken root in her mind, and all the circumstances attending her quitting the hotel in New York where he had left her.

He was amazed when she related Mrs. Farnum's instrumentality in the matter. It had never occurred to him that she could have been connected with it, although he had known that she was in America at that time.

He was furious upon learning how she had garbled the account of his cousin's engagement to Margaret Stanhope, and how his sister had purposely misrepresented facts in order to accomplish their separation.

He understood at once the whole plot, and recalled many things which went to prove that her ambition for him and her unreasonable prejudice against Virgie had been at the root of the whole matter.

"Did she dare write such falsehoods?" he cried, as Virgie repeated some passages from her letters.

"Yes," she replied, "I copied both letters. I knew that some time there would come a day of reckoning between you and me, and although every line had been burned into my brain, as if branded there with a hot iron, I was resolved that you should have all the evidence against you, and know whence my information came."

"Have you those copies with you, darling?"

"Yes; they are in my trunk."

"Will you go and get them for me? I want them now," he said, with a pale, set face.

Virgie left the room to comply with his request, but returned almost immediately with an envelope and a package in her hands.

"These are the letters—both are inclosed in one envelope," she said, "and this is something that belongs to your sister, Lady Linton," and she handed both to him.

She then told him how strangely her uncle had become possessed of that package so many years ago, and how she had but recently discovered to whom it belonged. She desired that he would now take charge of it and return it to her ladyship.

"It must be something very important for Miriam to be unwilling to trust it in the house during her absence," Sir William remarked, as he examined the seal and read the sentence penned upon the wrapper.

He laid it carelessly upon his knee, while he drew the copies of those miserable letters from their envelope.

But in so doing he changed his position slightly and the package, which a moment before he had laid down, tumbled to the floor.

It struck on a corner and the wrapper, which was old and brittle, burst from end to end, revealing a book about six inches long by four wide, which flew open midway as it escaped confinement disclosing pages closely written in Lady Linton's own hand.

"Ah! a diary, I judge," said Sir William, as he stooped to pick it up.

Then he gave a violent start as a few words caught his eye, and every atom of color fled from his face.

Lady Linton wrote a very bold, almost masculine hand, and it would hardly have been possible for anyone to be so near the book and not catch something written there.

The words which the baronet saw were under the date of August 15, and read thus:

"Another letter from that girl in New York."

He lifted his glance for an instant to Virgie—hesitated, then resolutely bent his eyes again upon the page and read on, while Virgie wondered at the act.

"* * * * Will she never have done sending her whining, nauseating love-missives to W?" said the diary. "My patience is exhausted watching the mail bag, lest by some chance he should get one, and all my nicely laid schemes be upset just as success seems so sure."

He turned a few leaves, glancing with lightning-like rapidity over them until he came to another entry that arrested his attention.

"The plot has worked to a charm, Myra says she accepted the whole story for a fact, and believes W. really untrue to her. She claims though that the child is legitimate, and says she will yet prove it. She threatens divorce—not wishing to hold a man unwillingly bound, ha! ha! If she will only carry out that project, my heart will be at rest."

Still further on he read:

"The girl has gone—disappeared, and no one knows whither. Her last letter was really quite tragic, but, thank fortune, it was the last; she said it was a final plea, but the paper writhed and seemed almost like a thing of life as I burned it; it nearly gave me the horrors. But I can afford to suffer a few stings for the sake of keeping that low-born girl from disgracing the house of Heath. W. will get over his moping by and by, and marry again befitting his rank; but if he does not, why, Percy and Lillian will be the gainers."

The book dropped from Sir William's nerveless fingers at this point, for a terrible passion was raging within him as the heartlessness, the treachery and cunning of his sister were revealed. He understood everything now; he realized how his sister had schemed and plotted the ruin of all his hopes, out of spite against the innocent girl whom he had married, and in the hope that he would choose a wife from the English aristocracy.

Surely Mark Alexander's prophecy had come true, for that mysterious package had indeed proved useful to Virgie in this crisis of her life. Sir William was amazed, shocked, and moved to fearful anger at his sister's daring wickedness.

She had robbed his mail bag for months, intercepting both his own and his wife's letters. She had also been guilty of falsehood and treachery of the worst kind, hardening her heart against his sufferings, ignoring the agony of a beautiful young wife and mother, and all the while eating his bread, educating her children at his expense, and lavishly spending his money to gratify her own extravagant tastes and whims.

"Will, dear, you positively frighten me! What troubles you? Your face is terrible to look upon," Virgie said, laying her hand gently upon his arm to arouse him from the stern reverie into which he had fallen.

He started at her touch, took the fair hand and raised it lovingly to his lips, while a smile, that was like sunlight after a tempest, broke over his face.

"I believe I was in a terrible mood, my darling," he said, "but you will not marvel when I tell you all that I have read; no, I will not tell you," he added, "it would be cruel to make you live over the past again as you would if I should reveal all my sister's treachery to you. Suffice it to say that all our sorrow has been the result of a cunningly devised and—yes, a fiendish plot that originated in her brain. Under ordinary circumstances I should regard a diary as something sacred to its owner, but the few words that caught my eye as I picked the book up made me feel justified in reading more.

"But, Virgie," Sir William concluded, sternly, "I shall never forgive Miriam Linton for the ruin which she wrought eighteen years ago."

Then he read the letters, and his ire grew hotter and fiercer until he came to that portion where lady Linton sent the money to Virgie and advised her to "go away to some quiet place, where she was not known, and might be able to bring up her child in a respectable way, so that its future might not be hampered by its mother's mistakes."

At this point, his anger reached a white heat.

Sir William dashed the paper to the floor, his face one crimson sheet of flame, and pressed to his breast the woman he so passionately loved.

"My poor, wronged darling, how dared she write such horrible things of you?" he cried, in a shaking voice, "and to send you that paltry hundred pounds! What must you have thought of me, to be guilty of such a dastardly act, after taking away all the fortune that your father settled upon you? I wonder your love did not all turn to bitterest hatred. Oh, Virgie! Virgie! I feel as if I could not bear it, even though you are all my own once more," he concluded, great drops of agony starting out upon his face.

"Don't, Will," she whispered, clinging fondly to him, "it is all over now; let us forget it, if possible, and enjoy to the utmost our new-found happiness."

"Forget! I can never forget. I will never forgive this terrible wrong," he said sternly. "Oh, my love, nothing can give us back those lost years; nothing can ever make me forget that for more than eighteen years I had a lovely daughter and never once looked upon her face to know her as such. Miriam Linton is a sister of mine no longer."

CHAPTER XXIV.
"GOD IS GOOD."

"To think," continued Sir William, after a moment of thought, "how systematically she set about her dreadful work, how remorselessly she persisted in it until she had achieved her end. And Mrs. Farnum! how she could see and know you, my beloved; how she could look upon that innocent darling, in whom was centered the hopes of both of us, and lend her aid, is a marvel and—a shame upon the name of woman! She shall never cross the threshold of Heathdale again."

"I cannot understand how she could have lent herself to such a base intrigue!" said Virgie, thoughtfully.

Sir William smiled bitterly.

"What is it, dear?" she asked, remarking it.

"I suppose I can give a reason, although it may sound somewhat egotistical," he returned. "Sadie Farnum—now Lady Royalston—once aspired to become Lady Heath, while it was the dearest wish of both her mother and my sister, who have been life-long friends, that I should marry her."

Virgie flushed. She could now understand why she had been the object of their curious glances when they first came to the —— Hotel, New York.

Sir William leaned forward and touched his lips to her crimson cheek and murmured:

"But I never saw but one woman whom I could be willing to have reign as mistress in my home. Virgie, I shall take you to Heathdale immediately."

Her whole face was dyed scarlet in an instant.

"You forget," she faltered, humbly, "I have no right to go there. I have forfeited all title to your name and home."

"I did forget," he answered, growing pale and sighing heavily. "I cannot realize since I have found you but that you belong to me now as in those early days; and you do; before Heaven, you are as truly my wife to-day as you ever were. But," and his arm closed tenderly about her, "the only obstacle is a legal point, and that is easily removed. You wish it, do you not, my darling? You will come to me at once?"

"I should die if I lost you again," Virgie cried, clinging to him with another burst of tears. "It has been a weary struggle to live without you all these years. But for Virgie I would gladly have laid down the burden long ago."

"Then may I go to London immediately for a special license, since we must conform to the letter of the law? I can never be separated from you again," said Sir William, as he fondly wiped her falling tears.

"But how can I leave my uncle, Lord Norton?" Virgie asked, suddenly remembering that new claim upon her and her promise not to leave him while he lived.

"Lord Norton your uncle? Ah, that accounts for your being here. I could not understand it," returned the baronet, looking astonished and remembering for the first time where she was.

Virgie explained how the relationship had recently been discovered, and informed him of his lordship's wishes that she should remain with him for the present.

"We must respect the wishes of a dying man," Sir William gravely replied, "and I, too, had forgotten my own obligations to him."

He told her all the circumstances of his cousin's accident and the summons that had brought him thither; of his proposal to try and complete the manuscript of Lord Norton's book, as, of course, Mr. William Heath would not be able to resume his work for a long time, and his lordship was liable to pass away without having his heart's desire accomplished if he attempted to wait for his recovery.

So it was finally agreed between them that they would wait at least until the completion of the manuscript before taking any steps for their reunion. They would see much of each other every day, while Sir William thought it would not be liable to create quite so much excitement in society if it was announced beforehand that he was soon to marry the niece of Lord Norton.

He declared, however, that his sister should know nothing beyond that fact until their return to Heathdale; but Virgie was so happy in being reunited to the love of her youth that she was almost willing to overlook and forgive Lady Linton's instrumentality in her previous suffering, and even to invite her and her family to be present when their new ties should be solemnized.

But Sir William was inexorable.

"No," he said, sternly; "it shall come upon her like a thunderbolt out of a clear sky. She has always wanted me to marry, and doubtless she will be jubilant when I announce my intentions; then she will imagine her triumph over you complete, and she shall not be undeceived until she sees you enter our future home as its mistress, for, of course, she will never dream that you and Lord Norton's niece are one and the same person; hers will be a double punishment when we all get home."

"Double! how so?" Virgie asked.

"It has long been her desire to marry Lillian to Rupert, my ward; but it seems, my darling, that he has chosen our daughter to be his wife. How strange it all seems," he concluded, thoughtfully.

"How did you learn so much?" Virgie inquired, with some surprise.

"The young gentleman himself came and told me a couple of days ago; he said he considered it his duty to inform me; but, let me tell you, my sister's disappointment will be no light one when she learns the fact," Sir William answered, all unsuspicious that her ladyship had learned the secret at the same time that he was informed of it.

"Does Lillian care for him?" Virgie asked.

"I am afraid she does," was the sober response.

"Poor child," sighed Virgie, regretfully, "and I am really sorry for Lady Linton's disappointment."

"Can you so readily forgive my sister, Virgie?"

"I believe I can, Will; I truly desire the spirit of forgiveness even for the great wrong that she has been guilty of; and, since nothing can ever again mar our trust in each other, I do not wish to cherish bitterness toward anyone. I am truly grieved for Lillian; she is not accountable for her mother's faults, and I have suffered too much, in believing another had usurped my place in your heart, not to feel a deep sympathy for her in losing Rupert."

Sir William sighed.

He regretted Lillian's unhappiness too, for he was very fond of her. She was a bright, beautiful girl, and for years had been the light of his home; and he believed, away from her mother's influence, she would make a noble woman. Still it was a matter for rejoicing with him that the young man whom he loved as a son would soon become a son indeed.

Virgie's meeting with her father was quite touching. Her mother had never told her who he was. She had shrunk more and more from the ordeal as the time drew near when it must be revealed.

She had intended telling her the morning following Lady Dunforth's reception when she had so unexpectedly learned that Sir William was Rupert's guardian, and she would have done so but for Mr. Thurston's visit, his startling revelation of her relationship to Lord Norton, and their sudden departure from London.

She was glad now that she had delayed the communication, for when she now made it, she could soften the otherwise shocking intelligence by telling her that all the past had been but a cruel mistake, which at last had been explained and rectified—that her father was a true and noble man.

Virgie came in from her walk just as her father and mother were speaking of Lillian.

"There comes Virgie," said her mother, starting up. "I must go to prepare her for her meeting with you."

"How much does she know?" Sir William asked, paling a trifle.

"Dear Will, she does not yet even know her own name, nor who her father is. I *could* not tell her, although I had promised to do so soon," Virgie explained, with quivering lips.

The baronet bent and touched them softly.

"I am glad, my beloved, that you have not told her; the shock will not be so severe now. Go, dear, but send her to me as quickly as possible, for my heart yearns for her. I know now why her presence affected me so strangely the other evening."

He released her, and she glided from the room to meet her daughter just outside the door; another moment and she would have entered.

"Mamma, what is it?" the young girl exclaimed, as she read in her expressive face something of the great change that had come to her during the last hour.

"Come with me, dear; I have something to tell you," her mother said, and she slipped her arm about her waist and drew her into a small room opposite.

In as few words as possible she told her all that had occurred, and the name of her father—the name which she had so long withheld from her.

"Sir William Heath, Rupert's guardian, *my father!*" said the bewildered girl, looking utterly dazed by the startling information.

"Yes, darling. It is a romance in real life, is it not?—and one which will end more happily than such romances usually do," was the smiling reply, although there were tears upon the grateful woman's cheeks.

"That accounts for a great deal," said Virgie, musingly.

"Such as what, for instance?"

"Your strange actions the other evening when Rupert told you who his guardian was."

"Yes; I utterly lost my self-possession then. It was an unlooked-for shock, and I feared that matters were going to be terribly mixed when you came to marry Rupert. But, darling, we must not keep your father waiting; he is longing for you. Remember, he has never yet looked upon the face of his own child, to recognize her as such."

"But, mamma," Virgie began, a startling thought coming to her, "you are—you are not——"

Then she faltered and stopped, her face covered with confusion.

"'I am, and I am not,' is rather an ambiguous statement, is it not, dear?" was the arch retort, although her mother was also flushed as she caught her meaning. "I understand your trouble, dear," she added, more gravely, "and everything is to be set right in a little while. This reunion will soon be properly solemnized, and then we shall all go home together. Now go, and I will follow you in a few minutes."

She led the beautiful girl to the door, kissed her tenderly, and sent her to Sir William. Then she sped swiftly up to her own room, where, locking herself in, she fell upon her knees and sobbed out her grateful thanks for the great joy that had been sent to her that day.

Virgie, her heart all aglow with love and happiness, went straight to the library.

Softly opening the door, she put her flushed, beautiful face within, saying, with charming eagerness:

"Mamma says that—that my father is here."

Sir William turned at the sound of that sweet voice, his whole soul in his face, and held out his arms to her.

"Virgie! my child!" he cried, in a tone that thrilled her, and her heart instantly owned its kindred, without a doubt of fear.

She sprang to his breast, laughing and sobbing all at once, and his kisses were rained upon her upturned face.

"Oh, my baby, whom I never saw! my darling for whom my heart has yearned so many years! God is good to give both my treasures to me, so fair and loving," he murmured, fondly, while his own tears mingled with hers, and his chest heaved with the emotion he could not control.

"Papa!" Virgie breathed, with a tender inflection that touched him deeply; "to think that I have never been able to say it before, while I have hardly dared to speak of you at all, because of the suffering it caused mamma."

"How has she accounted for my absence, love?"

"She has always told me that you went over the sea and were lost. Only since coming to London have I learned that you were living."

"It was better so," the baronet murmured, with a sigh. "It was better to have you think me dead, than guilty of the unfaithfulness which she was led to believe of me. But, my darling," he added, holding her off and gazing tenderly into her fair, young face, "you are very like what your mother was when I first saw her, and it is no wonder I was so attracted toward you the other night at Lady Dunforth's."

"Were you?" Virgie asked, looking up eagerly; "it is very strange, but it almost seemed to me as if I had known you in some previous state of existence! The sound of your voice moved me deeply and I could hardly restrain my tears when you gave me your hand at parting."

"It was the instinct of natural affection. Oh! it is such delight to have found both my loved ones; and yet," he added, with a twinkle of his eyes, "I am afraid I am not destined to have the exclusive right to but one of them for very long."

Virgie blushed crimson and hid her face on her father's shoulder at this allusion to her engagement.

He raised it and kissed her softly on her lips.

"I shall not be inconsolable," he said, smiling, "for if I have to resign something of my claim upon you, I shall thereby secure a son whom I have always loved as such. Rupert is a noble fellow, and he shall have my heartiest blessing, also, when I give him my daughter."

Virgie looked up archly at these words.

"I think that you and Rupert must have a mutual admiration for each other," she said, "for he is very fond of extolling his guardian; and, papa, I believe— I think you are very nice, too."

Sir William laughed. It was very sweet to find her so fond; he had feared that, never having known what it was to have a father, she would be shy and reserved at first.

"There will be mutual admiration between you and me if you say such pleasant things," he returned, with another caress. "How much you are like your mother!—the resemblance grows upon me constantly," he added, gazing closely into her lovely face, "all save your eyes; those, I think, are very like mine, my pet."

"Yes, and mamma has always told me that they are the dearest thing about me for that reason," Virgie answered.

Sir William turned to gather his other Virgie into his embrace—she having entered at that moment—a happy smile on his lips at this fresh evidence of her faithfulness to him.

CHAPTER XXV.
THREADS GATHERED UP.

Lord Norton was at once informed of the romantic incidents connected with his niece's early life, and while he sympathized with the trials and sorrow to which she had been subjected, he also expressed his gratification that all had ended so well, and she would henceforth occupy so proud a position.

He appeared to have conceived a great affection for her during the little time she had been with him, clinging to her as if she had been his own daughter, while she devoted herself tirelessly to him, doing everything in her power to make his last days peaceful and comfortable.

He lived only three weeks after she went to Englewood, but that was long enough to see the desire of his heart accomplished; for Sir William worked diligently upon his manuscript, completing it in about two weeks, and thus the aged veteran had the satisfaction of knowing that he would give to the world a valuable historical work to perpetuate his name when the world should know him no more.

The week following his death, and after the obsequies were over, Sir William wrote that letter to Lady Linton, announcing his contemplated marriage with Lord Norton's niece.

He purposely withheld nearly everything from her, save the bare facts that he was about to give Heathdale a mistress, and that she was the relative and heiress of his lordship.

He would have insisted upon having their reunion solemnized immediately if his cousin, Mr. Heath, had been considered wholly out of danger, while Virgie pleaded that it would hardly be proper, following so closely upon her uncle's death.

She went at once to Mrs. Heath upon being released from her own duties in the sick-room, to express her sympathy for her in her trouble, and the two women instantly became the warmest friends.

Mrs. Heath at once recognized Virgie as the beautiful woman whom she had met several years previous at Niagara. She was deeply wounded upon learning how she had been deceived regarding her marriage, and how she had suffered when they met, believing her to be the wife of the man who had wooed and won her.

"I loved you even then," she said, with starting tears, "though I wondered why you appeared so strangely at first. I wonder now how you were enabled to conduct yourself with so much self-possession."

Virgie and her playmate of that olden time renewed their acquaintance with evident pleasure, though the maiden could hardly realize that the stalwart, but rather bashful young man, to whom she was introduced as the "Willie" of long ago, was the same with whom she had enjoyed such childish freedom and shared her toys in the corridor of that great hotel in America.

Rupert was invited to come to Englewood the week following the funeral of Lord Norton, when he was greatly astonished to learn of the strange sequel to the story of his guardian's early life; and yet, a dim suspicion of something of the kind had been floating in his mind ever since that evening when Mrs. Alexander had been so unnerved upon learning that Sir William was his guardian; for he had known that there had been some deep sorrow connected with his past, and, having learned Mrs. Alexander's story, it seemed not unlikely that the two were in some way associated.

On the day that Virgie had encountered Lady Linton in Oxford street she had come to London, Sir William and Virgie accompanying her, to spend several days, having found it necessary to make a few purchases and some changes in her wardrobe before going to Heathdale; so it will be readily understood why the happy woman was at that time so unmoved by her ladyship's warnings and threats. Her heart was too full of joy and gratitude to allow of her feeling anything save pity and sorrow for her enemy, for she knew but too well that her evil deeds would all recoil upon her own head.

It was fortunate for their plans, however, that her ladyship did not meet her brother. He had accompanied his beloved to the store, where, after fastening that one lovely half-blown Lamarque rose in her mantle, he took leave of her for awhile; and went to attend to some business for himself; thus his presence in the city was not even suspected by Lady Linton. As soon as Virgie could be released by her dressmaker they all returned once more to Englewood.

By the 21st of the month Mr. William Heath was so far advanced toward recovery that his physician consented to allow him to be present at the ceremony, which was to occur in the church at Chester, and afterward to accompany the bridal party home to Heathdale.

At ten in the morning Sir William led the woman of his deathless love once more to the altar. Virgie and Rupert stood beside them as they renewed the vows of their youth, while Mr. and Mrs. William Heath, with their family, the Duke of Falmouth and his household, were also present to witness the ceremony.

The rector had been told something of the history of the couple upon whom he was to pronounce this second nuptial benediction, and his words to them were very solemn, very touching and impressive; and then the reunited husband and wife went out from his presence filled with a deep and holy joy such as they had never hoped to realize again in this world, while their future prospects seemed but the brighter for the chastening they had endured.

At noon the whole party left Englewood for Heathdale, followed by the congratulations and good wishes of the duke and his family, with whom Sir William and Lady Heath had formed a delightful friendship, and promised themselves much pleasure in the future interchange of visits.

Sir William and his wife experienced a slight feeling of dismay upon finding Heathdale all ablaze with light, and a brilliant reception in progress.

He had imagined that his sister, all unsuspicious of whom he was to bring home, might be there to meet him. He rather hoped she would, for he felt that Virgie deserved the triumph of coming to take her position there in her presence; but he was not quite prepared for a formal reception.

"I fear that Miriam has killed the fatted calf, and made a feast in view of our coming," he said, as they drove up the avenue.

"But, Will, it will be hardly the thing for me to receive your friends in my traveling dress," Virgie remarked, in a dubious tone.

"How long will it take you to make a toilet?" he asked.

"Half an hour will be ample time."

"Very well, then, while the rest of the party are received at the main entrance, we will drive around to a side door, slip up to our rooms, and send word that we shall be happy to greet our friends at half-past eight. Rupert, will you engineer the matter for us?"

Rupert gladly undertook the commission, and we know with what success, as well as all that occurred later, when Sir William appeared before the astonished company with his wife, whom they had previously known as Mrs. Alexander.

On the following day Lady Linton was so ill that she was unable to leave her room. The shock she had received, and the terrible restraint to which she had afterward subjected herself, was too much for her strength, and she was utterly exhausted, while her proud spirit was crushed to the earth.

Lillian was also in a very unhappy state of mind, although, to her credit be it said, she exerted herself, for her uncle's sake, to make everything as pleasant for him and Lady Heath as she was able to do under the circumstances.

She had spent the night in serious thought, and had wisely resolved to make the best of what she could not help, and in spite of the pain in her heart over her disappointed hopes, she was won by the beauty and sweetness of Rupert's betrothed, and after a day or two spent in each other's society, it was safe to predict that the two young girls would eventually become firm friends.

On the third day after his return Sir William visited his sister in her own room, and had a long and serious talk with her, deeming it wise to come to some understanding regarding their future relations without further delay.

She knew by the expression on his face, the moment he entered her presence, that she had nothing to hope from him; that he would not spare her for her part in the vile plot which had caused the misery of his past life.

He made a brief but very comprehensive statement of the whole matter, charging her with all her treachery and falsehood and crime, and she was forced to acknowledge her guilt.

But when he gave her the diary, portions of which he had read, and she saw that it had been examined, something of her old haughty spirit and arrogance blazed forth.

"Talk to me of falsehood; she told me that the seal had never been broken," she cried, with bitter scorn, a spot of vivid scarlet settling upon each sallow cheek.

"And she told you nothing but the truth, Miriam, for the seal was unbroken when she gave me the package to return to you. My wife has never read a single line that is written there. No one knows anything of its contents save you and me," Sir William replied, sternly, and then told her how he had happened to discover the nature of its contents, after which he felt justified in reading enough more to confirm the suspicions that one line had aroused.

"You have proved yourself a very unwomanly woman, Miriam," said her brother, with cold gravity. "Your nature, aside from the affection which you have for your children, is wholly selfish; it has become warped—degraded. You have not only hardened yourself against all honor and sisterly affection, but you have committed the most reprehensible crimes to further your miserable schemes.

"The wrong you did my young wife years ago, the insults you offered her, the falsehood and even theft of which you were guilty in sending that hundred pounds to her, the intercepting of our letters, are things that I can never overlook."

"Do you dare to accuse me of theft?" interrupted Lady Linton, bridling. "You gave me that hundred pounds for charitable purposes."

"I gave you that hundred pounds to use for the poor girl who was injured in that railway accident, and you stole it to add insult to injury. You mocked and scorned a woman who was your superior in every way—in whose veins there was as good blood as in your own, notwithstanding your boasted preëminence, and I grow cold with shame and horror every time I think of that paltry sum that you sent her, when I had brought back thousands of her money with me to England. Mr. Alexander left a small fortune to his daughter and I have had it in my possession ever since."

Lady Linton looked up aghast at this information. It was the first she had ever heard of that matter.

"You begin to appreciate something of what I have suffered," he continued, as he noticed the look, "but you can never begin to realize the misery which you brought upon two loving hearts so long separated; and to think that for more than eighteen years I was a father and never once looked upon the face of my child. Miriam, I can never overlook it. You have forfeited all respect from me, all claim upon me, and Heathdale can no longer be your home— you must go elsewhere to live, for I will not subject my wife to the constant companionship of one who has done her such irreparable wrong."

"William Heath, will you turn me out from my home, where I was born?" cried the miserable woman, almost fiercely.

"Your home?" he returned, severely. "For how many years have you cheated my dear ones out of *their* home—out of the love and sheltering care which should have been theirs? While my wife was toiling to earn her own support and to make provision for my child, you were spending money which rightfully belonged to them, with a lavish, almost reckless, hand, and rearing your children amid the luxury of which you had maliciously deprived them. I have family pride enough to provide for your needful support, for I cannot see you suffer; so I will fit up Fernleigh Lodge for your use while you live, and settle upon you an annuity of two hundred pounds——"

"Two hundred pounds!" interrupted Lady Linton, in a tone of horror.

"Yes. With economy, that will be sufficient for your individual needs," replied Sir William, coldly.

"I will give Lillian as much more until her marriage, when I shall hope to add something to the sum."

His sister's face was almost convulsed with rage at this announcement. She had never imagined any descent in the world so dreadful as this. She had spent three times the amount now offered her in a single year upon her own wardrobe, and now she was expected to provide her whole support out of two hundred pounds.

"Do you suppose Lillian and I are going to be able to live on a paltry sum like that?" she demanded, with quivering lips.

"My wife and child lived on far less than that for years, after you succeeded in ruining her faith in me," was the stern response. "It was no sum settled outright upon her, either; she had to *toil* for it with her own hands. She was not only the provider for the household, but nurse, and governess, and seamstress as well; while *your* children had their maids and tutors, to say nothing of the bills which I have paid sewing-girls and milliners for them. We will reverse the order for a while, and the sum that I have named will have to answer your purpose, unless your fertile brain can invent some way to increase it."

Lady Linton groaned at this inflexible verdict, while she writhed beneath his cutting words as if under a lash.

She could no longer shine in society, for there would be no means for providing the necessary accessories—dresses, jewels, laces, and the hundred other things she so dearly loved and had always had for the simple asking.

Her brilliant daughter, too, who had been so admired in the gay circles they had frequented, would have to drop out of her orbit now and be forgotten, while there would be no opportunity for her to make a distinguished marriage, which had been the acme of her mother's ambition.

"What will the world think? William, how can you be so cruel? It will blight all Lillian's prospects," she sobbed.

"If by blighting Lillian's prospects you mean that Lord Ernest Rathburn will give her the cold shoulder, it will be a good thing to have them nipped in the bud, for the fellow is devoid of both brains and principle, and has absolutely nothing but his plethoric purse to recommend him to anyone. I would much prefer to have her never marry than become the wife of such a coxcomb. As for your charge of cruelty, I must say it ill becomes you to make that complaint; you have been very extravagant during the last few years, and the study of economy will not harm you; besides, it is no more than right that *my* daughter should now enjoy the full benefit of her inheritance, which your children have so long usurped; not that I regret anything that I have done for them, for they are both dear to me, and I shall always be deeply interested in their welfare. Will you go to Fernleigh, Miriam?"

She would have been glad to reject his offer with scorn, but it was Hobson's choice with her—that or nothing.

Doubtless Percy would have offered his mother and sister a home, when he was settled, but his estate was yielding him comparatively little as yet, and she was far too proud to accept favors at the hands of his wife.

"I suppose there is nothing else for me to do," she wailed, and Sir William arose to leave her, uttering a sigh over this new evidence of her total selfishness.

He lost no time in fitting up the lodge, which was a small but cozy and convenient house, about five miles from Heathdale.

Virgie very kindly interested herself in all the arrangements, for Lady Linton would not make a suggestion or express a wish. When consulted upon any point she assumed an injured air, and remarked it was of no consequence— they could do just as they saw fit.

It was really a pleasant home when all completed, and Lillian thanked her uncle and Lady Heath most heartily for their kindness, and seemed quite interested in the domestic details of their small establishment.

In three weeks from the time of Sir William's return, Lady Linton took possession of Fernleigh, a sadder if not a wiser or a better woman, and there she literally buried herself, making no visits, and denying herself to all callers.

Lillian, however, showed a much better spirit, and tried to look upon the bright side of their condition. She was growing very fond of the new occupants of their old home, and was often invited to visit Heathdale, and when Harry Webster at last came, for his long-promised visit to Rupert, she did not fail to recognize the young man's superiority over her old admirer, Lord Ernest, while Mr. Webster's admiration for the brilliant brunette was very marked from the first.

In less than three months it was formally announced that Lillian Linton would, in the following fall, through her marriage to Mr. Webster, become a naturalized citizen of America, the country which she had once affected to so despise.

Mr. Knight and his sister paid Lady Heath a visit in March, and were overjoyed to find all her sorrow at an end and the future looking so bright.

They were persuaded to remain until after the marriage of Rupert and Virgie, which was to occur about Easter.

A grand wedding had been arranged, and after a tour on the Continent the young couple were to reside at Englewood for a portion of each year and spend the remainder with Sir William and Lady Heath at their town house in London.

Lillian was invited to officiate as chief bridesmaid, assisted by the Misses Huntington and the Duke of Falmouth's eldest daughter, while, of course, Harry Webster was to be "best man."

The ceremony occurred in the fine old church at Heathdale, which was crowded with the elite of the country for miles around, for a report of the beauty of the heiress of Heathdale had spread far and near.

Sir William gave away the bride, and the gift was accompanied with his heartiest blessing.

Virgie, in her bridal robes, seemed the "fairest that e'er the sun shone on," and no one looking into her dark eyes, so full of a calm, trustful joy, or noting the fond, proud smile upon her young husband's face, could doubt that these were

"Two souls in sweet accord,

Each for each caring and each itself unheard;

True to truth, nor needing proof nor proving,

Sure to be ever loved and ever loving."

There was a brilliant reception afterward in the grand old mansion of which Sir William was so justly proud, and the servants were heard to declare that a finer wedding had never occurred within the memory of the oldest among them.

As Virgie came down stairs, after exchanging her bridal dress for a traveling suit, Sir William met her in the hall and drew her into the library for a last few words. He put a package into her hands; and then, drawing her to his breast, he said, with great tenderness:

"My darling, this is your marriage dowry, to be used just as you choose, and I am sure of its being wisely used; but remember that you are to come freely to your father if at any time you particularly wish for anything. All that I have is yours. I live but for you and my other Virgie, and Heathdale is your inheritance."

[THE END.]

Milton Keynes UK
Ingram Content Group UK Ltd.
UKHW031047120324
439302UK00006B/513

9 789357 944892